PROTECTED BY THE WOLF PRINCE

JESSICA GRAYSON

ARIA WINTER

Purple Fall
Publishing

Published in the United States by Purple Fall Publishing. Purple Fall Publishing and the Purple Fall Publishing Logos are trademarks and/or registered trademarks of Purple Fall Publishing LLC.

Identifiers:

ISBN: ebook 978-1-64253-040-7

paperback 978-1-64253-068-1

Cover Design by Kim Cunningham of Atlantis Book Design.

PRINTED IN THE UNITED STATES OF AMERICA

CHAPTER 1

LUNA

The light of the harvest moon spills in through my bedroom window, bathing the room in a silver glow and filling me with dread. I push the door open and step onto the balcony, casting my gaze to the gardens below.

The sound of raucous music and laughter carries on the breeze, and I lift my eyes to the path, beyond the wall. Lined with several rows of fine stone houses with tiled roofs, the cobbled streets are full of people making their way to the city square. In the distance, the orange glow of the harvest bonfire is easily visible.

My heart is heavy as I study a few couples whirling and dancing around the flames and the silhouettes of the bystanders, wondering if Malak is there among them. This is an important celebration for his people, and I imagine he has looked forward to this day all year.

Whereas I have prayed for it to never come. Nonetheless, it is finally here, and I am miserable beyond words.

Movement below the balcony catches my attention, and I squint my eyes into the darkness as if that will somehow help me to see better. A cool breeze blows through the gardens, lifting a few stray tendrils of my long, red hair before I gently tuck them back behind my ears. I pull my heavy cloak around my shoulders, warding against the chilled air as shadows dance below.

I shake my head softly, mentally chastising myself for my overactive imagination as the branches rustle and vines sway on the wind like living curtains. There is nothing down there. It is merely my eyes playing tricks on me, I'm sure.

"Psst." The sharp noise carries up from below, startling me abruptly.

Piercing green eyes blink up at me from the darkness, a moment before Malak peels away from the shadows. I place my palm to my chest, directly over my racing heart, and breathe out a sigh. "Thank goodness it's just you."

"Just me?" Moonlight glints off two rows of sharp, white fangs as he flashes a wolfish grin. "Who else did you think it might be?"

He jogs forward a few steps, and then effortlessly leaps up onto the balcony. He swings his legs over the railing and then he's standing before me. His masculine scent fills my nostrils, and the heat of his body radiates to mine. Before I can stop myself, I lean in and breathe deeply of the heady smell of earth and forest. I love the way he smells.

My heart flutters as his green eyes search mine with a piercing gaze.

He runs a hand through his windswept, short black hair, revealing the pointed tips of his ears. He's dressed only in black pants, but they are probably not real. As a Wolf-Shifter, he is able to conjure the appearance of clothing. The silver moon carves his body in shadows and light, illuminating his broad, muscular shoulders, strong arms, and

2

the thick planes of muscle that cover his abdomen and chest.

It does something strange to me to be so close to him now, knowing that he is probably nude standing here. Despite the fact that I am human and he is a Wolf-Shifter, we've been best friends since we were ten. These past few years, however, I've found myself wishing we could be more.

My gaze travels over his handsome face, from his heavy-set, dark brows, his aquiline nose, and sharp, angular jaw covered with just a hint of stubble.

"I did not expect you," I tell him, a bit breathlessly. "That's all."

"Where else would I be?" He cocks his head to the side. "We always watch the fireworks together during the harvest festival, Luna."

My heart clenches as the memories of all our younger years flood my mind. It's our yearly tradition to observe the fireworks from my balcony.

He regards me a moment before stepping closer. So close that my entire body hums at his nearness. "I thought you might wish to go to the bonfire this night." A hint of a smile tugs at his gorgeous mouth. "We are old enough now to partake in the festivities."

Heat floods my body as I wonder just which festivities he means. Does he mean the supposedly harmless dancing around the fire, that sometimes leads to couples sneaking away together into the dark, or does he mean the rite of passage observed by his people when they come of age? The mating chase that takes place in the forest tomorrow, beneath the light of the full harvest moon.

As I'm pondering this, he leans in and drops his head to the curve of my neck and shoulder. I inhale sharply as he skims the tip of his nose along my sensitive skin and breathes deep. "You smell divine," he whispers, his breath

3

warm with a soft hint of mint. "Like apple pie and cinnamon."

While others might find this strange, he has done this since we were young. The first time was when I returned to the capital after having visited with my grandmother back in Avalor for a few months. We were ten. I thought nothing of it at the time, beyond that it was a bit strange, but lately… each time he does this, my entire body flushes with warmth.

My pulse pounds in my ears as he lifts his intense gaze to mine, and then licks his full, perfect lips. "Perhaps I should have a taste," he says, his voice smooth and deep.

He wraps his arms around me and tugs me to him. Playfully, I hit at his shoulder. "You most certainly will not." I laugh, wriggling in his arms as I pretend to try to get away. He is always teasing me like this.

A wolfish grin overtakes his features, accentuating his sharp fangs.

"My, what big teeth you have," I gently admonish.

"The better to eat you with," he growls, and I laugh and squirm even more at the ticklish sensation as he tightens his hold and nuzzles at my neck, pretending that he's trying to bite me.

The light sting of his fangs prickles my flesh, and we both still. My chest heaves against his with each breath, and my pulse pounds not with fear, but with desire.

We remain frozen in position for a moment, suspended in that awkward place between friendship and… something else we have yet to acknowledge or name.

He pulls back just enough to study me with his intense gaze. His eyes drop to my mouth and warmth pools low in my belly as he leans so close, I can almost taste the soft mint of his breath. "Luna, I—"

"Malak!" I recognize his brother—Fredrik's—voice immediately. "Come on! Let's go to the bonfire."

I take a small step back, trying to hide my disappointment at the interruption.

Fredrik looks up at us from the garden below, and waves at me. "Hi, Luna!" Although he is only two minutes older than Mal, they are hardly twins. Fredrik has brown hair and gray eyes, whereas Mal seems to have inherited his mother's features. "Are you going to join in the festivities?"

Before I can answer, Malak yells back. "Go on, Fredrik. I'll find you later."

"Fine." Fredrik rolls his eyes. "But if you do not hurry, all the good ones will be spoken for," he calls over his shoulder as he leaves.

Dread twists inside me because I know he's referring to the Wolf-Shifter females who have come of age this year, just as they have. They turned nineteen two months ago, three weeks before I did.

Malak turns back to me. "Do you want to go?"

The last thing I want is to watch him dancing with other women. Besides, my father already forbade me to go to the bonfire. "Father will not allow it."

"What about the chase tomorrow?" he asks. "Will you be there?"

"I'm human, Mal." I frown. "The chase is for Wolf-Shifters."

"Humans participate sometimes," he counters. "They—"

"I cannot," I tell him. "If Father will not let me go to the bonfire, he certainly would never let me participate in the chase."

His expression falls. "How will you find a mate then?"

My heart clenches. The purpose of the chase is to find a mate, which means that Malak will find someone tomorrow. Someone that isn't me.

I lower my gaze. "Like most human women in my position, I suppose." My Father is the Ambassador from Avalor, and we have lived in the kingdom of Winterhold since I was ten. Due to my father's prestigious position and wealth, and the fact that my mother is a distant cousin of Avalor's king, he has already had many requests for my hand. "My parents will arrange for my betrothal to whomever they deem most suitable."

Malak's eyes flash with concern. "Do you want to be bound to a stranger?"

"Not particularly," I say, unable to hide the bitter edge to my tone. "But it is how these things are done."

"Do you truly not have a choice?" he asks.

"If I were not nobility, I would be free to choose whomever I wanted, but with titles come expectations and responsibilities." I repeat my mother's exact words to him. "It is how it is done."

"That is barbaric," he exclaims.

I frown. "Is your brother not held to the same?"

He shakes his head.

"But Fredrik is the eldest," I point out. "He will be King of Winterhold someday."

"It is still his choice who he takes as a mate," Malak says. "Just as it is mine. That is why we have been looking forward to the harvest moon." His lips curl up in a faint smile. "To participate in the chase."

I only have a vague idea of what happens during this event, and although I am loath to think of him with another, I have to know. "How do you choose someone in the chase?"

"Some go by instinct alone, their inner wolf guiding them." He shrugs. "But others go into the chase already having decided upon who they want, and the chase is merely a formality... a rite of passage in the choosing."

Even though he is the second son, and younger prince of Winterhold, Malak has no shortage of female admirers. I wonder if any have caught his attention.

"And once you choose that person?" I ask. "What then?"

His eyes snap to mine, his gaze intense. "Are you asking me the details of the claiming?"

Heat flares my cheeks. "I—I was just curious." I stumble over my words. "I—"

"I will tell you if you truly wish to know."

Despite my embarrassment, I give him a small nod.

"While in their *wolven* form, a female will signal her interest by locking eyes with a male while they circle one another. If she decides she does not want him, she will then growl and move on to someone else. But if she is still interested, she will encourage him to give chase. Once he catches her, they will shift back into their two-legged form. She will accept him into her body, and he will give her his claiming mark on her neck, sealing the mate bond between them."

I've lived around them long enough to know that Wolf-Shifters think nothing of nudity, nor of speaking so bluntly about coupling, but it is still a bit shocking to hear about the mating ritual. But my shock quickly gives way to concern. Malak will be partaking in the chase. Tomorrow night, he will be in the woods choosing a mate. The knowledge is like bitter poison in my heart.

He takes my left hand, studying it intently.

"What are you doing?" I ask, curious.

"When a human desires to claim a mate, he gives her a ring, does he not?"

"Yes."

"And if she accepts it, then others who see that ring will know she is taken."

That's a simple way to look at it, so I nod.

He stares at my hand a moment longer before lifting his gaze back to mine. "Come with me to the bonfire, Luna."

"My father will not allow it."

"He does not need to know." Malak tilts his head to the

7

side, training his left ear toward the door, brow furrowed as he listens. "He is asleep and snoring. So is your mother."

A smile crests my lips. "My, what big ears you have," I tease him about his wolf sense of hearing.

"The better to hear you with." He grins in return. "Now, let's go."

He hoists me to his chest. My heart slams in my throat as he steps onto the railing. "Mal," I whisper, giving him a warning glare. He knows I hate it when he jumps from high places. Especially when he's carrying me.

"I've got you." He flashes a devilish grin, and then leaps off the balcony.

I bite back a shriek and close my eyes, bracing for the worst.

Gently, he nuzzles my cheek, and I open them again to find us already on the ground. I was so nervous, I barely felt the jostle when we landed. "You are safe with me, Luna," he whispers. "I would never let anything happen to you."

"I know," I reply softly. My heart clenches as I stare up at him. Tomorrow, he might be mated to someone, and I can hardly stand it.

If I don't want to lose him, I must be brave and tell him how I feel. If I do not, I'll regret it forever. Determination fills me. It is now or never. I must tell him tonight.

* * *

WHEN WE REACH the town square, a band is playing loud and cheerful music while dozens of people dance around the bonfire. I stare in awe as the Wolf-Shifters and a few humans dance with complete and utter abandon.

This is nothing like the elegant ball at the castle last winter, when Malak's father entertained the King of Avalor. Mal and I danced then, and it was the most romantic night of my life. We stayed awake and watched the sunrise together. A wistful sigh leaves my lips. I have dreamed of that night so many times since then.

"Come on, Luna." He takes my hand and pulls me into the throng of people.

At first, I feel a bit awkward, but as I gaze at everyone around us, I realize that this is a night of fun and revelry. I doubt anyone will judge me here.

I grasp my dress and lift it just enough that I can dance freely, without worry of entangling myself as Mal and I join in. My skirt sways with the music and my hair falls free of my braid as I laugh and dance with Mal to the lively music.

I'm breathless and panting, but I don't want to stop. I'm having so much fun that my cheeks hurt from smiling. Mal lifts me into his arms as if I weigh nothing, spinning me around before setting me back on the ground at the end of the song. He takes my hand and pulls me off to the side as we catch our breath.

Several couples walk toward the entrance to the city gardens, only a few steps away. Mal and I follow after them. It's dark, but the moon provides just enough illumination that I can make out the path as he guides us to the hedge maze, near the center. "Do you remember the time you thought we were lost in here?" he whispers softly.

"We *were* lost." I laugh.

"No, we weren't." He tips up his chin. "A Wolf-Shifter *never* gets lost."

"Is that so?" I tease.

"It is," he says proudly. "We have superior sight, hearing, smell, and—"

"Then come find me." I push away from him and break into a sprint, turning one corner and then another as I make my way through the maze.

All the while I can hear him behind me, his feet crunching

on the gravel as he gives chase, laughing and calling out. "You cannot run from me, Luna," he teases. "I will find you."

Wolf-shifters are much faster than humans, and I know I only have a few moments before he catches up with me as I hear him give chase. We started this harmless children's game of hunter and prey when we were much younger, but over the past few years it has developed into something else.

Something that borders on the forbidden because, every time we do this, my longing for him grows even more. I love the moment when he finally catches me in his arms, holding me close.

But he is a Prince of Winterhold, and I am merely an ambassador's daughter. Even if Mal wanted me, as I desire him, my father would never agree. Wanting someone I shouldn't is dangerous. And I know if I am not careful, it will destroy my heart.

Sometimes I feel as if there is a connection between us. An invisible tether from his heart to mine. I often fantasize that he experiences the same breathless anticipation I do when he races after me. That my feelings are not one-sided, as I fear them to be.

When I make another turn, I find an open area with a three-tiered fountain and a wooden bench beside it. I hide behind the bench, crouching low.

Malak skids to a halt when he reaches the fountain, and I put my hand to my mouth, trying to stifle my breathing.

"You think you're so clever," he teases. "But I can hear your heartbeat, Luna. You cannot hide from me."

Stifling a laugh, I jump up from my hiding place and make a run for the exit, but his strong arms wrap around my waist, stopping me in my tracks.

He tugs me to him, the front of his body flush against my back. His breath is warm on my neck as he whispers. "I caught you. You're mine." Desire coils deep within. "Do you yield to me?"

"No." My voice comes out a breathless whisper. He skims his nose along the curve of my neck, growling low in his throat. I have never surrendered easily, but I want so much to surrender now, here in his arms.

He says wolves can smell things like fear and desire. With his sensitive wolf nose, I'm worried my body will give me away. So, I wriggle in his hold, managing to free my arms to reach back and exploit his only weakness, tickling his ribs.

Laughter bursts from his lungs, but he quickly pins my arms to my sides, locking me in an iron embrace. I twist my neck to look back at him, arching a teasing brow. "My, what strong arms you have."

He narrows his eyes, but I notice the hint of a smile that plays on his lips. "The better to hold you with."

He loosens his grip again, and I turn in his arms to face him. He is so handsome it takes my breath away. My gaze drops to his full, perfect mouth. Something about this moment makes me bold, and I reach up and touch his cheek. "Mal," I speak softly. "There's something I want to tell you."

CHAPTER 2

MALAK

Luna's warm brown eyes stare up into mine as she touches my cheek. She is the most beautiful female I have ever seen. And as her gaze holds my own, my inner wolf howls beneath the surface, desperate to mark her, claim her, and make her ours.

I cannot deny that I desire this more than anything, but I can't give in to these primal instincts. Not yet. Luna is not a Wolf-Shifter. I must court her as a man, not a beast.

Although my inner wolf and I are one and the same, he is unsettled and will remain that way until we have claimed her. He knew she was ours the moment we met. I was too young to understand it at the time, but as we grew older, I recognized what my wolf knew from the beginning: Luna is my mate, and my heart and soul will only ever belong to her.

My control begins to slip, and I pull her flush against my body. Her delicious scent of apples and cinnamon floods my nostrils. Her cheeks flush a lovely shade of pink as I run my hand through her red hair. Gripping the long, silken strands between my fingers, I tug gently, tipping her face up to mine. "What is it?" I ask softly.

The smell of her desire is unmistakable as she stares up at me, softly biting her lower lip. The soft scent of mint escapes her mouth, fanning across my lips, and I lower my gaze to the curve of her mouth. I want to know if she tastes as good as I've imagined. Searching her eyes for silent permission, I lean in to close the small gap between us.

Someone cries out, startling her, and she quickly pulls away as a couple runs past, giggling as they race around the corner.

The clock bell tower strikes five times, and she gasps. "I have to get back, Mal. My father will be awake soon."

Curse the time and curse her father. Ambassador Falen is unreasonably strict and has never approved of our friendship. I'm convinced that the only reason he purchased a country manor in Westry, the next town over, was so that he could keep Luna away from me as much as possible. He sends her and her mother there almost every weekend.

It is bad enough that he sends her away for the summer to stay with her grandmother, back in Avalor. Those months have always been torture for me, counting down the days until she returns.

As the ambassador from Avalor, one would think her father would want to encourage a relationship between his daughter and a prince of Winterhold. Instead, he seems intent upon keeping us apart. Our two kingdoms have come close to war several times. Luna is distantly related to Avalor's king. If she will accept me as her mate, I only hope that her father will recognize the political advantage of such a match, even if he does not approve otherwise.

"Do not worry." I lift her into my arms, and I love how she instinctively curls into me. "I will get you home before he awakens."

Tucking her close to my chest, I race down the cobbled streets until I reach her home. The garden gate is still unlocked, so I quietly slip back inside. She squeezes her eyes shut and tenses as I leap up onto the balcony railing.

Gently, I nuzzle her head and she opens them again and gives me a smile that melts my heart.

The golden light of dawn is a thin line across the horizon as I set her back on her feet. Quietly, she opens the door to her room.

"It's the last day of the festival," I remind her. "We can get some of those apple tarts later that you love so well."

She smiles, but it doesn't touch her eyes.

"What is wrong?" I ask.

Luna gives me a hesitant look before lowering her gaze. "Do you already have someone in mind that you would like to chase?"

"Yes," I reply without hesitation, and her eyes snap up to mine. A smile crests my lips as I study her lovely face. "I have wanted her for a long time now."

Her expression falls, and she looks away again. "Oh." She swallows hard. "Does she know how you feel?"

My brow furrows deeply. Does she truly believe I am referring to someone else? How can she not know it is her that I speak of?

I open my mouth to declare my intent, but she pushes away before I can answer, turning her back to me. "Never mind," she murmurs. "I—I don't want to know."

Hope sparks in my chest. This is how she behaves when she is jealous. I saw it once before when she thought Drulisa was flirting with me. And if Luna is jealous... that means she dislikes the idea of me with another.

With her back still to me, I take a step closer so that there is barely any space between us. I lean in, and she shivers slightly as my lips brush the shell of her ear. The delicate

14

scent of her arousal floods my nostrils as I whisper. "How is it that you know everything about me, and yet... you do not know my heart's desire?"

She turns to face me, tears brightening her eyes. "Mal, I need to tell—"

"Your mother is coming," I hiss under my breath, recognizing the cadence of her steps on the floorboards as she approaches.

"She is rarely ever up this early." Luna frowns. "Are you sure?"

I gesture to my pointed ears and tip up my chin. "My superior wolf senses never lie."

"Luna, dear?" her mother's voice calls softly from out in the hallway. "Are you still asleep?"

Luna rolls her eyes. "Not anymore, Mother," she says, trying but failing to hide the irritation in her tone. "I'll be right there."

I notice the bolt is engaged on her door, so her mother cannot simply barge in, thank the goddess.

"You and your pointed ears," Luna teases, and I give her a sly smirk as I make my way to the balcony.

Carefully, I slip through the door, pausing a moment to look back at her. "I'll return in a few hours," I whisper. "We can enjoy the last day of the festival together."

She nods and I close the door behind me. Grabbing the edge of the railing, I swing my legs over the side and drop down to the garden. The moment I hit the ground, my senses go on high alert.

Quickly, I crouch behind a nearby shrub. My ears prick up as I recognize the scent and the sound of Luna's father's voice. Ambassador Falen is often loud when he speaks, but right now he sounds markedly agitated, and I wonder why.

Peering through the foliage, I observe as he paces back and forth, waving his hands animatedly toward a man I do not recognize. Falen appears disheveled, and his face is nearly as red as his hair as he gestures angrily toward the house. "You have no business coming to my home," he shouts. "My wife and daughter are here."

"I am the High Mage of the King of Avalor," the other man says. "*He* is the one who sent me because *you* are not doing your job as instructed."

"I am *working* toward peace," Luna's father counters. "And I have been for the past nine years." He shakes his head. "You will undo all of it. If you fail, you will only succeed in provoking King Darak into war," he says, referring to my father. "Mark my words."

My curiosity is piqued, and I quietly move closer as I continue to observe. It is strange that King Brenor would send his High Mage here, when it is well-known that my father despises them. He considers most Mages just as dangerous as Blood Witches. The ones he does tolerate, he refers to as a necessary evil.

"Wolf-Shifters are aggressive, protective, and extremely territorial," Falen presses. "King Darak is likely to kill you as soon as you cross the threshold of the castle."

"You always speak of his inclination to violence." The Mage waives a dismissive hand at him. "And yet you are still standing here, alive and breathing, are you not?"

"Because I understand King Darak's limits and how much I am able to press our agenda while still maintaining the peace between our two kingdoms," Luna's father states firmly. "He hates Mages. If you think he will grant you an audience, you are wrong. Trust me: You are making a mistake. I have been in this position for years, and I—"

"You've been asleep at your post," the Mage says darkly.

Falen's head jerks back. "What are you talking about?"

"Your daughter," he says. "Do you know that she spends time with Prince Malak?"

"They are friends," Falen says dismissively. "What of it?"

"Did you know she stayed out with him last night at the bonfire?" Luna's father blinks several times, and the man continues. "I lost track of them after they snuck away into the city gardens together, and into the hedge maze."

"What?" Her father's face reddens even further. "I—I do not believe this. Luna knows I forbade her to go to the bonfire. And she most certainly would never do anything that might compromise her honor."

My claws extend as ice-cold rage floods my veins. How dare this man spy on us. I will rip him apart.

"She was there. They both were," he insists. "He's a Wolf-Shifter. His father will not condone a relationship with a human. If you do not want her honor questioned, then I suggest you do something about this situation immediately before rumor spreads that she is a Wolf-Shifter's bi—"

"Enough!" Luna's father shouts. "I'll not have you speak of my daughter like this. Do you understand?"

A low growl rumbles deep in my chest. My inner wolf rages beneath the surface, demanding that we rip this man apart, limb from limb.

"Leave!" Her father gestures angrily toward the garden gate and out to the street. "And *do not* come back. Do you understand?"

The man narrows his eyes. "Perfectly." He walks toward the gate and slams it shut behind him, disappearing into the city.

Luna's father runs a hand roughly through his hair and grits his teeth as he stalks back toward the house. Anger is easily read in his features, and I cannot bear the thought of any of it directed at my mate. I will not leave her to face him alone.

"Ambassador!" I call out, sprinting toward him from the bushes. "Wait!"

He spins to face me, his eyes wide. "What are you doing here?" Panic flits briefly across his expression. "How long have you been here?"

Judging by his question and the worried look in his eyes, I know better than to answer that honestly. "I only just arrived."

His shoulders sag forward slightly before he narrows his eyes. "Why are you here, Prince Malak?"

A plan forms in my mind. It's not ideal, and I have not discussed it with Luna, but I am relatively sure she feels the same for me as I do her. It's a risk I must take. Especially if I want to shield her from her father's wrath. If her father is concerned that my intentions toward her are dishonorable, I will put that to rest right now. "I have come to ask for your daughter's hand."

His jaw drops.

I meet his gaze evenly. "I understand you are entertaining offers for betrothal, and I would like to submit my own."

When he does not answer right away, I wonder if perhaps I am doing this wrong. "This is... how humans choose their mates, is it not?" I cock my head to one side. "I was under the impression that this is the way it is done among your kind."

"It is. But you are not human, Prince Malak. Surely you understand that such a pairing is not... ideal."

"It is not unheard of for Wolf-Shifters to take human mates," I point out. "I may be a second son, but I am still a prince of Winterhold. As such, when I turn twenty-one, I will become High Lord of the Vale and its territories. As my mate, Luna would become the High Lady and she would have a comfortable life, and—"

"No," her father cuts me off once more. "I'm sorry, but I will not give you my blessing."

I stare at him in shock for all of a second before the blinding rage of my inner wolf floods my veins, turning my vision red. "And what if she chooses me?" I challenge. "Would you not consider her wishes when it comes to a mate?"

"It is *not* her decision," he states firmly.

"It is *her life*," I grind out. "It is not for *you* to dictate who she will spend it with. If I ask her for her hand, and she accepts me, would you truly refuse her choice?"

He blinks several times. "You have not asked her yet?"

"No." I would have if not for the interruption this morning when her mother came to her door, but I do not tell him this. To do so would confirm what his companion told him earlier: that she was out with me all night.

Her father opens his mouth as if to speak, but instead clamps it shut again. He lowers his gaze, brow furrowed deeply as if in contemplation before he finally returns his attention to me. "I will consider your proposal."

Cautious hope builds in my chest as I scan his face. My father has always warned that cunning is second nature to Ambassador Falen. That his neutral expression is the perfect mask for his shrewd and calculating mind.

"I'd like to see Luna," I tell him, but he steps in front of me, blocking the entryway.

"Come back at noon," he says. "We will speak then."

I bite back a rumbling growl. Everything within me demanding that I storm past him and go straight to her room. She is mine, and until I claim her, my inner wolf will never be settled. Even now, fierce possessiveness burns in my veins.

Luna's father does not know it yet, but if she will have me, it matters not what his decision may be. I will claim her as my mate whether he accepts it or not.

CHAPTER 3

LUNA

"We have much to do," Mother says as I yawn loudly. "We will go to the seamstress first so she can take your measurements."

I'm exhausted, but I cannot tell her why. So instead, I sip on my morning tea, hoping it will give me a bit of energy to stay awake. "Why?" I ask. "I already have enough dresses, Mother. I'm hardly in need of more."

She purses her lips. "We'll be returning to Avalor after the winter solstice. Your father has already asked your grandmother to reopen the rest of the manor in preparation for our arrival and for your coming out ball."

My heart stops. "We're going to Avalor? For how long?"

"Indefinitely." She takes another sip of her tea, staring at me over the rim of her cup. "Your father has taken a position as personal advisor to the king."

"But… our life is here," I protest. "We've been here since I was ten years old. I—"

"It has been a long time, but now we can finally go home, Luna."

"This *is* my home." Worry floods my veins. I don't want to leave Winterhold. Malak is here, and I—

"Where were you last night, Luna?" my father asks in a thunderous voice as he storms into the room.

Mother spins to face him. "Falen, what is the meaning of this?"

He ignores her as his iron gaze locks on mine. "Answer the question," he demands. "Tell me the truth."

"I—I went to the... bonfire last night, Father." Mother pales as Father's expression grows even angrier. "I'm sorry. I merely wanted to join in the festivities. I—"

"Were you with Prince Malak?"

Panic trips my heart. I don't know how, but he knows already. He is merely waiting to see if I'll lie to him, so I have no choice but to tell him the truth. "Yes," I reluctantly admit. "I was."

He clenches his jaw. "Did you go into the city gardens with him? Into the hedge maze?" he asks, his voice rising.

"I—"

"Tell me!"

"Luna, darling," Mother says, worry etched in her features. "Surely, you did not—"

"Nothing happened between us," I deny vehemently. "I swear. Malak is my friend. We—"

"Pack your things." Father cuts me off. "Now!" he roars.

"But, Father!" I look to my mother for help, but her eyes are full of tears.

"Oh, Luna, you'll be ruined if anyone finds out," she cries. "No one will want to—"

"No one will find out," Father snaps. "We're leaving the city. Now."

"Nothing happened!" I snap. "I swear it!"

"You think your suitors will care to listen, if rumors begin to circulate?" he grinds out. "Wolf-Shifters do not place value on virtue, like our people do." His face grows even redder with anger. "They think nothing of dancing nude around a bonfire and then sneaking away in the dark with a lover. But you are human, Luna—a citizen of Avalor, no less. You are held to a different standard. You are *not* a Wolf-Shifter, and I'll not allow your honor to be ruined by one. Do you understand me?"

I know my parents were raised in Avalor with its strict traditions and beliefs about virtue and honor and purity before marriage, but we've lived in Winterhold for almost a decade. It should not be a scandal for an unmarried woman to be seen at a festival with an unmarried man.

"Father, you're being ridiculous!" I protest. "Wolf-Shifters mate for life. They do not bed others for sport or leisure. I swear to you: nothing happened between—"

"Get packed!" he snaps. "Be ready to leave in one hour!"

"An hour?" Mother asks incredulously. "We cannot be ready that quickly. We need at least half a day to—"

"There is no time," Father snaps. "Do not question me, Melara. Just do as I say. Please," he says, softening his tone. "You must trust me." Father turns his attention back to me. "I am doing this for all of us."

Biting my bottom lip to keep it from quivering, I blink back tears. I have been wrongly accused and I'll not allow Father to see me cry. "I know I should not have gone to the bonfire, but I swear to you that nothing happened between me and Malak." I hold his gaze evenly. "Malak knows I'm human, and he respects Avalor traditions, Father. He would never compromise my honor."

"And yet he did," Father says darkly. "And in front of several witnesses too, by taking you into the hedge maze alone, Luna. Can you not see that?"

"That was not his intent," I protest. "Malak is a good man."

"He is not a *man*," Father counters. "He is a *Wolf-Shifter*."

"Who are these witnesses?" I ask. "What are they claiming to have seen, exactly?" I challenge. "I would face my accusers instead of allowing them to spread vicious and unfounded rumors about—"

"It does not matter."

"It *matters* to me," I state firmly.

"Do not argue with me, Luna. Just do as I say." He turns to my mother. "We will stay in the country home for the next few weeks. Just long enough for any rumors to fade away. Then, we will return."

I don't want to leave. Not now. But I also know that there is no winning an argument with my father. If I deny him now, he would probably send me back to Avalor, to my grandmother, even sooner than the end of winter.

At least this way we will only be gone a few weeks. When we return, I will speak with Malak. I'll tell him how I feel. I have to. Time is running out. We will leave at the end of winter and I don't want to go without speaking the truth that resides in my heart.

I make my way to my room and begin packing. When I'm finished, I write a letter to Mal, telling him where we are going. At a glance, it appears simple enough, but it is not.

Mal and I have a system. A secret code we made up when we were children, playing at being spies. As an ambassador of a neighboring kingdom, all of the correspondence, including mine, had to be approved before being sent. So, I would always embed a secret message in each one, that only Mal knew how to decipher.

Feeling bold, I decide not to hold back. After I'm finished, I read the coded part again to make sure I did it correctly.

Dear Mal,

I have something important to tell you, but it needs to be in person. If I could, I would participate in the chase. With you. If you feel anything more than friendship for me, I'm asking you to wait for my return.

Yours always, Luna

Heat flares my cheeks, and I swallow hard as I stare at the secret message. Drawing in a deep breath, I steel my courage and fold the paper.

I hand it to one of the servants and brace myself for another argument when he gives it to Father's assistant—Radagar—for approval.

Even though I've always thought it ridiculous, I understand that each correspondence must be approved. It is a condition placed upon my father by his superiors.

Radagar smooths a weathered hand through his short, white hair as he scans the note, which simply states that we are going to the country house for a few weeks. He gives me a small nod before allowing the servant to continue.

Worry tightens my chest. I only hope that when we return Mal will not have found a mate during the chase this night.

CHAPTER 4

MALAK

By the time I reach the castle, I've already gone over what I'll say to Father at least a dozen different ways. I know that I'm expected to participate in the chase tonight, but I do not want to. There is no point if Luna will not be there.

Two guards bow low as I approach the heavy wooden doors of the throne room. "Is my father inside?" I ask.

"Yes, my prince," one of them answers.

He turns to the other and they each take one of the heavy metal latches and pull on the massive doors to open them. I study the scrolling patterns etched into the wood of a pack of wolves howling at a full moon, set against a star-covered sky, trying to determine how best to approach my father with my news.

When they are fully opened, I lift my gaze to find Father seated at the far end of the room on his ornately carved throne etched with gold. My mother sits beside him on the smaller one. I hate that it is this way. A queen is supposed to be equal to the king here in Winterhold, but it was a condition set by my Father's father—my grandfather—when he approved their bond.

Mother was born of the leader of a rival pack that makes their home in the mountains to the Northwest—the territory known as the Vale. Their bonding ended the fighting between them. But my grandfather always worried it would undermine his own pack to allow her to rule as equal to my father—his heir.

And because this was agreed upon, it cannot be undone. A Wolf-Shifter's word is tied to his honor. Once given, it cannot be rescinded for fear of facing the wrath of the moon goddess. If I were my father, I never would have agreed to such a condition in the first place.

As I approach the throne, Father's gray eyes fall hard upon mine. "You were out with the ambassador's daughter last night."

"Yes." I will not deny it. "Luna is my friend. And I would make her my mate, if she will accept me."

Father's eyes widen and Mother goes pale beside him.

"You cannot bind yourself to her, my son," Father states firmly.

"Why not?"

"Because she is the daughter of Ambassador Falen." He leans forward. "I do not trust him."

"What does that have to do with *her*?" I ask incredulously. "Do you think she'd be her father's spy? That she would work to overthrow your power? That she would—"

"I *will not* chance it," he grinds out.

I snap my gaze to Mother. Her hair is raven-black, like mine, marking her as an outsider—part of the Vale Pack that my grandfather was so worried about. "You bound yourself to a member of a rival pack," I point out. "And yet in all these years, Mother has never tried to overthrow you."

Father growls low in his throat. "That is different."

"How?"

"Your mother is a Wolf-Shifter. Luna is human. A citizen of Avalor, at that," Father practically spits out the word.

He hates Avalor. The only reason he tolerates Luna's father is because he wants to avoid a costly war between our kingdoms. He does not trust them. He never has, and I doubt he ever will.

"Luna grew up in Winterhold," I protest. "She—"

"The answer is no," my father snaps. "And that is final."

"Your father is right, Malak." Mother gives me a pitying look. "Besides, the chase is tonight, my son. You can find a proper mate there."

"Proper?" I ask. "What is that supposed to mean?"

"A Wolf-Shifter female," Father lashes out. "*Not* a human female."

"Is it that she is human?" My brother Fredrik's voice sounds behind me. "Or is it that she is from Avalor? Which is the problem?" he challenges. "Because I thought it was our right to choose who we take as a mate."

I turn and smile at my brother, glad for his support. Fredrik claps a hand on my shoulder as he comes up beside me. He stands tall and proud, a younger version of our father with his short, brown hair and gray eyes.

Father growls low in his throat, baring his fangs. "It is both," he says darkly. "I will not have an Avaloran in our pack. Nor will I tolerate a human."

"There are many Wolf-Shifters who take human mates," I counter.

"Humans are weak compared to our kind," Father snarls. "I will not allow you to muddy our line with half-human offspring."

"She is mine," I growl.

My muscles ripple beneath my skin, preparing to shift into my wolven form as my inner wolf howls in protest at my father's words.

"My inner wolf has already chosen her," I grind out. "*I* have already chosen her. She is mine."

"What?" Father stares at me in shock. "This cannot be right. She cannot be your fated mate."

"She is," I insist.

"Her father will never agree to such a match. Neither will I."

"I did not ask for your blessing." I meet his gaze evenly. "If she will have me, I will claim her as mine."

"Then you will be exiled from our pack," Father says, and Mother gasps.

"So be it," I snarl and turn on my heels, stalking back to the doors and out into the hallway.

Fredrik runs up behind me. "Mal, wait!"

I turn back to face him.

"Just give it some time," he says. "Father will surely see that he is wrong. After all, he married Mother, did he not?"

"He will not change his mind, Fredrik. If she were not a citizen of Avalor, he might. But he hates them. You know he does."

"Yes, but—"

"Prince Malak," one of the servants calls out, walking briskly toward me. "I have a letter for you."

He hands it to me, and I recognize the wax seal immediately. Eagerly, I tear it open and scan the contents.

The plain message reads that Luna and her family are traveling to the next town over, to stay at their country home for a few weeks. A smile crests my lips when I read the hidden message she has encoded. The true one.

She wants me as her mate. I know she does. If she didn't,

she would not ask me to forgo participating in the mating chase.

I lift my gaze to Fredrik. "I need you to lie for me."

He frowns. "About what?"

"Tell Mother and Father that we are both going to the woods tonight for the chase."

"You're not coming?" he asks incredulously. "We've been looking forward to this all year."

"I know," I tell him. "But that was only because I thought Luna would be there also. I meant to claim her this night."

His mouth drifts open. "You do realize that you would have had to fight your way through several wolves to do so, right?" he teases. "Every male would have tried to entice her to be his."

I scowl at him, and he puts his hand up in mock surrender. "Not me, of course," he quickly adds. "She is my friend, and I know she is yours. But others," he points out. "She is desired by many."

My inner wolf bristles. "She is mine," I snarl.

"Then go claim her." He grins. "I'll lie for you on one condition."

"What is it?"

A sly smirk twists his lips. "That you name your first pup after me."

Playfully, I punch at his shoulder, and he quickly ducks out of the way, laughing.

"If Luna agrees to be mine, you'll have to ask her. I know better than to make a promise like that without consulting my mate."

His expression sobers. "Father will be furious, you know."

"Yes, but hopefully, he'll get over it." I shrug. "I'm sure his father was upset when he and Mother decided to bond. And that worked out, did it not?"

Fredrik gives me a doubtful look. "I hope you are right. If

you're wrong, he will exile you from the pack." He claps a hand on my shoulder and meets my eyes evenly. "May all be as it should be," he says, invoking the blessings of the moon goddess."

"May all be as it should be," I reply solemnly before I turn to leave.

CHAPTER 5

MALAK

Although the town of Westry is less than two hours from the capital, it took much longer because I decided to travel off the main roads. Not that everyone in all of Winterhold would recognize me, but even a few would be damaging. Especially when I want my parents to believe I'm preparing to take part in the mating chase.

It is only a few hours until sundown, and I am so close to my prize I can nearly taste it. Thick fog and swirling mist wrap around my legs as I track my quarry through the dense forest. Closing my eyes, I focus on Luna's delicate scent. A cool breeze blows through the woods, carrying the delicious fragrance of apples and cinnamon. My heart rate quickens with the thrill of anticipation, my inner wolf instinctively responding to the distinct scent of she who is my mate.

A flash of red catches my eye in the distance and I pick up my pace.

It is her. I am certain of it.

The earth is soft and damp beneath my feet and my canines lengthen into sharp fangs as the desire to claim and possess what is mine threatens to consume me.

Up ahead, I notice a small stone building directly in the center of the bustling town square. The smell of fresh bread carries on the wind. I glance through the window and notice two bakers, a man and a woman, hard at work inside.

The man is shaping loaves, while the woman slides several others into the ovens. The bakery is bustling with activity. Several patrons line up inside as another man helps them at the counter.

A figure dressed in a red hooded cloak, carrying a wicker basket, walks up the steps and pauses at the doors. She pushes back her hood, and her long, silken red hair catches on the cool breeze.

My nostrils flare and my eyes nearly roll up in the back of my head as Luna's familiar scent floods my senses. Curling my hands into fists at my side, it takes every bit of my strength to remain rooted in place, forcing myself to remain concealed in the shadows along the edge of the town as she enters the bakery. As much as I long to go to her, I know I must wait.

My plan to surprise her will have been for nothing if I reveal my presence now.

A growl rumbles in my chest as the male behind the counter smiles brightly at her. I snarl as he looks her up and down while she peruses the various displayed pastries.

One of the other bakers—a woman with white hair tied back in a knot at the top of her head—comes from the back. She shoos the man at the counter away, and Luna reaches into her basket and pulls out a folded letter. The woman nods and then slips it into her apron. Luna gives her a few coins and the baker gives her two loaves of bread for her basket.

After what feels like forever, she finally exits the bakery. My mouth drifts open as I catch sight of her face. Long lashes frame warm brown eyes. She tucks a stray tendril of hair behind the shell of her ear, so dainty and round where mine is tapered at the tip.

Booming thunder rolls overhead, and a small crease forms across her delicate brow as she lifts her gaze to the sky. Her plush, pink lips part as she mutters under her breath, "Seven hells, will this rain never end?"

A smile quirks my lips. Luna hates the rain. She always complains that it ruins her hair.

She is dressed in a long, red skirt that matches her cloak and a simple white top with a dark leather corset. She quickly pulls the hood over her head to protect her from the rain and dashes toward the forest, holding tightly to her small basket.

I follow close behind her as she enters the dark woods alone. The last rays of the sun lengthen shadows from the trees as my ears detect the sounds of nocturnal creatures beginning to stir in their dens.

It is concerning that she does not recognize the danger of entering such a place by herself, and I am all the more pleased that I followed her here. If she were truly alone, there are things in this forest that might be tempted to hunt her. But because I trail her, nothing would dare. For any that sense me nearby would recognize that I am the superior predator in these woods.

And I would not hesitate to kill anyone who dared try to harm her.

The moon is nearly full, and my muscles ripple beneath my skin with want to change forms. I decide not to deny myself the pleasure, and allow the change to overtake me.

Besides, I can better guard Luna this way. With a quick whirl of wind, I shift into my four-legged wolven form. The

JESSICA GRAYSON & ARIA WINTER

delicious scent of apple pie and cinnamon fills my nostrils as I follow on silent paws, behind her. My black fur allows me to blend in with the fallen leaves and the tree trunks in the dark woods.

She stops abruptly and spins back, her warm brown eyes searching the darkness. "Who's there?"

Although I wish to remain hidden, I cannot deny how pleased I am by her heightened awareness of her surroundings. These instincts will serve her well to keep her alive. Standing there so fierce and unafraid, I have no doubt she will make a fine mother to our pups.

If only she will accept me.

She pulls a dagger from her belt, holding it out before her. "Show yourself."

Silent and still, I crouch low in the brush, observing as she finally turns back and starts on her path.

It takes everything inside me not to run toward her. To wrap her in my arms and claim her here in the woods, giving her my mark so that every male would know she is mine. But I know I cannot. Not like this. Luna is human. Their courtship and mating rituals are very different from those of my kind. Her letter said she would participate in the mating chase with me if she could, but I must know for sure that she wants me. I will not just assume.

Luna makes her way to her family's country home that sits in the center of a grand estate. The setting sun casts a warm glow over the gray and white stone facade. The house is enormous, with towering columns and a sweeping stairway leading up to the main entrance.

I observe as Luna walks up the steps and enters through a set of large, double wooden doors. I have been here once before, when I was fifteen. Luna spoke so often of this place that I wanted to see it. I slipped away from the castle and surprised her. We spent the day together wandering the woods. Because it is only a few hours outside of the capital, I returned home before my parents even knew I was gone.

Golden light spills out through the windows, and gray smoke rises from several of the chimneys along the roof. It is quite a walk from here back to the bustling town square of Westry, if one were to take the main road behind the house. That is probably why she cut through the woods.

Luna has a love of the outdoors and nature that rivals even that of my own kind. If she were a Wolf Shifter, I suspect she would spend most of her time in the forests if she could.

Carefully, I step from the shadows of the trees and make my way to the country manor. Slipping behind the garden wall, I slink through the finely manicured hedges until I reach the line of windows in the center of the structure that looks in on a large sitting area.

I peer inside, and notice several large, plush green velvet sofas and oversized chairs spread out before a massive fireplace with a roaring fire burning on the hearth.

Luna's mother—Melara—is seated on one of the chairs. Luna walks over to her. I'm always struck by how much they resemble each other, except for their hair. Her mother's is dark brown, whereas Luna's is red, like her father's.

I train my ears toward them, hoping to hear as they speak. Luna hands her the basket, pulling out the two loaves of bread.

"We could have sent the servants for those, Luna," Melara says.

"I know. I just... wanted to get some fresh air."

Her mother takes her hand. "Are you still upset, my angel?"

Luna swallows hard and then nods. "I don't understand why Father was so angry, Mother."

Melara shakes her head softly. "Your father is merely trying to protect you."

"From what?"

"From any vicious gossip that could ruin your prospects of finding a good husband," she explains, and I bite back a growl. "Your father has had several offers for your hand. If word were to circulate that you were seen sneaking off into the night with Prince Malak, it could ruin you."

"We did nothing wrong," Luna states firmly.

"Good," her father says. "When we return to the capital, you must distance yourself from the prince."

"Why?" she counters. "Malak has been my friend since we were ten years old."

"I forbid you to ever see him again."

"You cannot do that," she protests.

"I can and I will." He turns to her mother. "In fact, I think it might be best if you and your mother simply return to Avalor before winter, and I will follow after the new year."

Anger burns in my chest. Her father brought her here, hoping that I would not follow. That I'd stay behind and participate in the chase ritual and find someone else. He never intended to tell Luna about my proposal. Of that, I am now certain.

"I *will not* go," Luna refuses. "I'm nineteen. You cannot force me to leave. Besides, Winterhold is where I grew up. It's more my home than Avalor has ever been."

Falen's eyes widen briefly in shock before anger overtakes his features. "If you think to stay for Prince Malak, he is a Wolf-Shifter. His father would never allow him to marry a human. I am certain of it."

Rage twists deep inside me. It appears the ambassador knows my father even better than I do, and despite their contentious relationship, they seem to have more in common than they both think. Neither of them can abide the thought of their children choosing someone outside of their species.

"Besides," he continues. "The mating chase is tonight. With any luck, Prince Malak and his brother will each find a mate and that will be that."

Luna storms out of the room, and I quickly move to the side of the house where her bedroom is located. I remember it well, for the last time I was here, I snuck in while she was sleeping to surprise her.

I leap up onto her balcony, concealing myself in the shadows of the heavy vines covering the exterior wall of the house. The window is open just enough to allow in the cool evening air. It is lavishly furnished, with a large four-poster bed along the far wall, with a wardrobe to rival the size of my brother's. There is a table, and a sofa across from it that sits before a roaring fireplace.

Luna enters and then slams the door shut behind her. I reach up to tap on the glass but stop as her mother knocks on the door.

"Luna?" she calls softly. "Please, let me in. I want to talk to you."

"No. I want to be left alone."

One of the estate guards walks below the balcony and I duck beneath the window. Taking shallow breaths, I remain completely still, hiding in the shadows. Luna's father obviously dislikes me, and I'd rather not be caught before I can speak with her.

Once the guard passes, I glance in the window again, and observe curiously as Luna tiptoes to the door and carefully turns the handle, peering out into the hallway a moment before shutting it again quietly and turning the lock. She fastens her red cloak around her shoulders, and then turns to the window.

Quickly, I duck again, and when I hear it begin to lift, I

slip around the corner to observe from my hiding place, wondering what she is doing.

It is already dark outside as she makes her way to the gardens. Human night vision is poor compared to my people, but the full harvest moon provides enough light for her to travel without using her lantern until she reaches the edge of the dense woods.

Alarm skitters through me as she enters the forest. She must not realize the dangers that lurk in this dark place. Although it is close to the estate, and there are few creatures bold enough to hunt so close to a human establishment, I know there are some that would if they knew such a treat as her had ventured into their domain.

I follow Luna as she makes her way beneath the thick tree canopy until it opens up into a clearing. Several large boulders are arranged in a circle in the center.

Luna drops to her knees and sets the lantern down beside her. With her arms outstretched, she lifts her gaze to the sky. "Goddess of the Moon," she speaks softly. "I know I am not one of your children, but I come to seek your favor. Please, Goddess. Grant me that which my heart desires most."

My mouth drifts open as she recites the prayer I taught her long ago, when we were just children, and she had been so curious about the ways of my people.

She pulls a moonstone from her pocket and then carefully places it in the circle of boulders before rising to her feet with her lantern and turning back to the woods.

Still in my two-legged form, I follow closely behind her. When she is almost at the edge of the forest, near the estate, I purposefully step on a twig to alert her of my presence.

The sharp snap breaks the silence in the darkness, and she stills.

"Who's there?" she calls softly. "Show yourself."

Anticipation thrums in my chest as I sneak up behind her.

I lean close and whisper in her ear. "Did you—" She spins to face me, dagger in hand and the tip already at my throat before her eyes widen in recognition. "Miss me?" I finish.

"Malak?"

A sly smirk twists my lips.

"Seven hells!" She places her hand over her heart. "I almost stabbed you!"

CHAPTER 6

LUNA

Malak flashes his devastatingly handsome and rather wolfish grin. "Surprised to see me?"

"What were you thinking?" I ask, exasperated, tucking the dagger back in my belt. "I could have accidentally killed you, Mal."

"Killed?" He arches a teasing brow and makes a show of glancing down at his sharp, black claws. "I think not." He tips up his chin, straightening his shoulders. "I am a Wolf-Shifter. We are not easy to kill."

I stop short of rolling my eyes, trying to hide the smile that tugs at my lips.

He's much taller than me. The top of my head sits just below his chin. His glowing green eyes study me with piercing intensity as my gaze travels over his sharply pointed ears to his heavy-set, dark brows, his sharp nose and masculine jaw. It's difficult, but I force myself to bite back a sigh. He is the most handsome man I've ever seen.

He's dressed only in black pants, leaving his torso

completely bare. My mouth runs dry at the sight of his exposed upper half. With broad shoulders, a powerful chest, and chiseled stomach, his entire body is thick layers of solid muscle. Not an ounce of fat on him.

He loops an arm around my waist and pulls me close. His other hand tangles in my hair as his fingers grip the long, red strands to tip my head to one side, revealing my neck to him.

He skims his nose along the column of my neck, inhaling deeply as he scents me. "I missed you." His warms breath against my skin sends a shiver of pleasure down my spine.

A dark and woodsy scent—his distinctly masculine smell —surrounds me, and I melt against him. "I missed you too."

"It's dangerous for a tender morsel such as yourself to be wandering alone in the woods, you know," he teases.

I am perfectly capable of defending myself. "And just why might that be?"

"Because a big, bad wolf might be tempted to hunt you." He grins, flashing two rows of sharp, white fangs.

"Is that so?" A soft laugh escapes me, and I arch a teasing brow. "Well, he'd have to catch me then, first, wouldn't he?"

Before he can answer, I push at his chest and spin back toward the forest, running as fast as I can.

He's on me in less than a minute. A small yelp leaves my mouth as he bands his strong arms around my waist, and he bears me to the ground. My heart pounds, not from fear, but from intense longing as he pins me in place.

His body is a solid wall of muscle against my back. He nudges my head to one side with his jaw and a warm puff of air hits my neck as he scents me again.

"I caught you." His voice is smooth and deep in my ear. A low growl rumbles in his chest, and the vibrations move through me, sending a pulse of heat straight to my core. "Do you yield to me?"

I twist onto my back and grin up at him. "Never."

Even as the word leaves my mouth, I know they are a lie. Surrendering to him like this has been the subject of many daydreams and fantasies since I turned sixteen.

His pupils are blown wide so that only a thin rim of green is barely visible along the edges as he stares down at me with an almost predatory gaze.

This is relatively new. Only a handful of times over the past year has he looked at me in this way. I wonder if it is his wolf instinct, triggered by catching his prey, or if it is a sign of interest. I can never tell.

But there is no question that right now I am his prey and he is a predator. Every part of him speaks of raw power and primal strength, and yet... he is always so careful and gentle with me that I could never be afraid of him.

My heart hammers as his gaze holds mine intently. Heat radiates from his body to mine, and my gaze drops to his lips, wondering what it would be like to kiss him.

Although I know that I am human and he is a Wolf-Shifter, I cannot help but wish we were the same. Because if we were, perhaps we could be more to each other than we are now, instead of always walking this fine line between friendship and something... more.

"Why were you out here?" Gently, he tucks a stray tendril of hair behind my ear. "It is dangerous for you to be in the forest alone at night."

"I assume you received my letter," I reply, trying to avoid answering the question.

Wolf-Shifters are good at sensing lies, and he will know if I make one up about why I was praying to the Moon Goddess. A smile tugs at my mouth because she works much faster than I thought. I prayed for her to send him to me instead of having him participate in the mating chase back in Winterhold.

When his older brother, Fredrik, casually mentioned last

week that they were now old enough to participate, I was devastated. I could hardly bear the thought of Malak with someone else.

He nods. "I saw your prayer to the goddess," he says, and I wince inwardly. "What did you ask for?"

When I do not answer right away, he leans in and scents my neck again. As a Wolf-Shifter, I know his kind can tell much about another's emotions by their smell. Although, as I think about it, I've never seen him get as close to anyone else as he does to me. "Tell me." He gently nudges his jaw against mine in an affectionate gesture.

Feeling bold, I touch his face, and he pulls back enough to meet my gaze. As he studies me, all my bravery disappears, and I bite my lower lip, unsure what to say as indecision wars within me.

If I tell him the truth, this moment could change everything between us. And if he does not feel for me as I do him, then I will have ruined our friendship, and I cannot bear the thought of losing him. I'd rather have him as my friend, than to not have him at all.

"Luna, what is it?" he asks, concerned. He pulls me up to sitting. He leans against a nearby trunk and settles me across his lap. All of this: his touch, the way he looks at me, holds me, and cups my cheek to turn my face to his... it's all so familiar and easy between us. I've known him so long, and I do not want to risk—

"I overheard your father telling you to stay away from me," he says. "Is it something to do with that?"

I shake my head softly because it's so much more than just the conversation with my father. I'm in love with Malak, and I'm so afraid to tell him. I don't think I could bear it if he does not return my feelings.

"Has someone hurt you? Were you praying for vengeance?" A deep growl rises in his throat, and I force myself not to roll my eyes. Of course he would think this. He once told me that vengeance is one of the most common reasons for praying to the goddess of the Moon. "If someone has harmed you, I will end them," he says darkly. "I will rip their head from their—"

"No one hurt me."

"Then, what is it?" he presses.

"I'm afraid if I tell you, that you will look at me… differently," I finally admit, worried that I'm about to ruin everything.

His head jerks back. "I vow that I will not. Now, tell me." He brushes his thumb across my cheek. "You are my best friend. You know you can tell me anything."

Best friend. The words are sharp barbs in my already bleeding heart. "What if I wanted more?" I inhale sharply as the thought escapes my lips unfiltered.

"Your letter." His eyes search mine. "Is that what this is about?"

I avert my gaze, unable to look at him as the truth leaves my mouth. "I prayed that you would not participate in the mating chase in Winterhold."

He stills. "Why did you ask the goddess for this?"

Emotions lodge in my throat, and I cannot answer.

"Luna, look at me." His voice is gentle but insistent. "Please."

I lift a tear-filled gaze to his and the words come tumbling from my mouth, unbidden. "I cannot stand the thought of you with someone"—my voice hitches—"who isn't me."

His green eyes widen a moment as if in disbelief. "You desire me to be yours and yours alone?"

Swallowing hard, I steel myself and then nod softly.

A handsome smile curves his mouth, and he crushes his lips to mine.

My heart pounds in my chest, and pleasure coils tightly within. His kiss is not soft and tender as I'd always fantasized. It's even better: demanding and intense.

His fingers tangle in my hair, angling my face up to his. "I am yours," he growls fiercely as he stares deep into my eyes. "And you are mine, Luna."

Surprise parts my lips on a gasp, and he plunders my mouth, curling his tongue around my own. A small whimper leaves my throat at the delicious sensation as he explores my mouth, kissing me like a man possessed, devouring me with his lips and his tongue.

When he finally pulls back, my entire body is ablaze, and I'm breathless and panting.

He frowns. "How could you ever think I would want anyone but you?" My heart flutters. "Do you not remember the vow we made to each other?"

My mind drifts back to the summer when we'd turned sixteen. He chased me in the woods, as he always does, but this time, when he caught me, it was different. As if something were charged in the air between us as he scented my neck. Beneath the light of a full moon, he took both of my hands in his own.

His eyes searched mine, as they do now. So serious and earnest, as if staring deep into my soul. "Will you pledge yourself to me, Luna?" he asked. "Swear to me that you will take me as yours, when we are grown. Me, and no other."

"I pledge myself to you, Malak," I whispered solemnly in reply. "I will take you as mine. You, and no other."

"That was a lifetime ago, Mal." I frown. "We were young, and—"

"It was three years. Hardly a lifetime," he counters. "And we were not children then, Luna." His green eyes fix upon mine with piercing intensity. "We swore ourselves to each other."

Hope sparks in my chest. "What are you saying? That…

45

you meant it?" I ask cautiously, worried that I'm wrong and my heart will be shattered.

He traces his fingers lightly across my jaw and down my neck to my shoulder, leaving a trail of fire in their wake as he continues down the length of my arm before taking my hand in his own.

He lifts our joined hands, his dark eyes glittering in the moonlight as he presses a tender kiss to my knuckles. "You are mine," he says solemnly. "And I will take no other as my mate but you."

"What about our parents?" My heart simultaneously plummets and soars. As much as I want him, it's an impossible situation. "You are a prince of Winterhold, and I am... the daughter of an ambassador. Our fathers hate each other. Our kingdoms are constantly at each other's throats, and always on the brink of war."

"I do not care what my father thinks." He threads his fingers through mine. "I told your father that I wanted to ask for your hand."

My head jerks back slightly. "When?"

"Today," he says. "Before you left."

He was so desperate for us to leave quickly, and now I wonder if this was why. "He did not tell me," I murmur. "He said that you would probably find a mate this night, during the chase."

"I have." He gently squeezes my hand, and my heart fills with joy. "But I do not think your father approves."

"I don't care. But you are a prince, Mal. You have so much more to lose than I do. I'm not a princess or even a duchess. I—"

"Even if you were an Orc, it would not matter," he counters.

Laughter bursts from my chest, even as happiness bubbles

up within me. "An Orc?" I playfully hit at his shoulder and then tease him. "And what about a Troll?"

A handsome grin curves his mouth. "It still would not matter." He tugs lightly at the neckline of my sleep gown, and then rubs his jaw against the curve of my neck and shoulder on one side and then the other.

"What are you doing?" I laugh softly, wriggling in his hold at the tickling sensation.

"I am scent-marking you," he says matter-of-factly. He lifts his head, his gaze full of possession. "So other unmated males will know you are already taken."

"You know humans do not have a heightened sense of smell like your people do," I remind him. "So a human male would not know that—"

He pulls a small box out of his pocket and holds it out to me with a wolfish grin.

My mouth opens in surprise as I take it from him. "What is this?" I already have my suspicions, but I'm still afraid to hope. All of this is like a dream, and I worry that at any moment I will awaken in my bed alone.

"I came prepared," he says proudly, tipping up his chin. "Human males should recognize this sign that you are claimed."

With trembling hands, I open the box. Nestled inside is a delicate golden ring with a moonstone in the center in the shape of a heart. On either side of it are intricately carved wolves with a lovely scrolling pattern across them. It's the most beautiful ring I've ever seen. "You are serious about this," I whisper, more to myself than to him, my heart still suspended between happiness and disbelief.

"I give you my troth." His gaze holds mine as he slips the ring onto the fourth finger of my left hand.

Emotions clog my throat, and I cannot speak around them as I stare down at my ring.

He lifts my hand to his face, leaning into it as his thumb traces a pattern on the inside of my wrist. "Mine," he says, his voice a low, deep rumble as he closes his eyes and rubs his jaw across my palm.

"Yours," I reply, and his eyes snap open, dark and full of hunger.

In one swift motion, he rolls me onto my back, capturing my mouth in a claiming kiss.

I love the way his body covers mine, surrounding me in his warmth and his masculine scent. His tongue sweeps into my mouth as he deepens our kiss, both possessive and demanding all at once, and I feel as if I'm floating.

Only the barrier of my clothing separates our bodies. Malak rolls his hips against mine and the press of his hard length against my entrance creates a delicious friction between us, setting my entire body aflame. My heart beats wildly in my chest, as his sharp fangs nip lightly at my throat.

He reaches between us and gently pulls at the neckline of my gown to reveal my left breast. I draw in a shaking breath as the cold night air kisses my bare flesh. His warm hand cups the soft globe. When he rolls the already hardened tip between his thumb and forefinger, I moan as lightning arcs through me.

Encouraged by my response to his touch, he pulls the gown away from my other breast. I inhale sharply as he closes his mouth over the peak, laving his tongue across the sensitive bead.

My pulse throbs between my legs as desire coils tight in my core. "Mal," I barely manage, clutching tightly to his shoulders and then running my fingers through my hair as he continues his ministrations, worshipping my body with his hands and his tongue.

A low growl of arousal vibrates his chest as I pull him closer, desperate to feel his body against mine.

His hand travels lower, moving down my form. He grips the hem of my gown and pushes it up to my hips. His fingers trail fire in their wake as he glides them up my left inner thigh. When he reaches the lacy material between my thighs, he carefully pulls it aside, and I gasp at his touch.

"So perfect," he whispers against my heated flesh as he drags his fingers through my already slick folds.

"Mal." The breath rushing from my lungs as he traces his thumb over the sensitive pearl of flesh at the apex. "Mal, please."

He concentrates on that spot, and my entire body lights up as pleasure heats within. It's too much and not enough all at once. I've never felt anything like this before. Intense sensation builds deep inside me, and I can hardly catch my breath as my entire body goes taut like a bowstring.

And as much as I want him, I'm afraid. This feeling is too much. Too intense, and I feel as if I may drown if I allow myself to succumb. "Mal, wait," I pant as I wrap my hand around his wrist.

He stills and lifts his head. "Did I hurt you?"

I shake my head. "No, I just… I've never felt anything like this before and I—" I swallow hard. "I'm nervous, Mal."

He wraps his arms around me and rolls us onto our sides, facing each other. Mal runs his fingers through my hair. "We can stop," he whispers softly. "We do not have to do anything until you are ready."

I nod, and he gently pulls my neckline back up to cover my breasts and then tucks my cloak around my shoulders. I nestle into him, enjoying the feeling of his strong arms around me as I rest my head on his bicep.

He presses a tender kiss to my forehead and smooths a hand down my back.

I cup his cheek. "Can we just kiss for now?"

A handsome smile lights his face, and he arches a brow. "You like my kisses?"

I decide to tease him. "I think so, but I'm not sure."

His expression falls. I try but fail to suppress a grin, and he laughs. "Are you teasing me?"

I laugh softly. "Maybe."

He rolls onto his back, placing his hand over his chest. "You stopped my heart, Luna." He shakes his head softly. "I thought you were serious, and I was worried you'd never let me kiss you ever again."

I press my lips to his, and then smile against them as I whisper. "Maybe we should practice."

He growls and deepens our kiss, plundering my mouth with his tongue, making me dizzy and breathless as desire pulses through my veins.

With my skirt still bunched up around my waist, I can feel the hard press of his length against my lower abdomen as he holds me close. Curious, I reach between us, and a tortured groan leaves his mouth as I explore him.

Warm liquid beads from the tip of his crown, and he's so large I cannot reach my fingers entirely around his girth. Several hard ridges band around his shaft. A large bulge of spongy tissue around his base swells and tightens beneath my touch. "My *stav* is very sensitive." He groans. "My knot even more so. If you keep—" His breath hisses out from between his fangs, and he grips my wrist, quickly pulling my hand away.

He rolls me beneath him. His stav is still hard and erect against my inner thigh, and warm liquid weeps from the tip, leaving a wet trail along my tender flesh as he kisses me fiercely, curling his tongue around mine and stealing the breath from my lungs.

I hold tightly to him, tracing my fingers along the thick cords of muscle that line his shoulders and back.

He rips his mouth from my own and presses a line of kisses along my jaw and down the curve of my neck. "Want to mark you as mine," he rasps, as his tongue traces over my already sensitive skin.

I tilt my head to one side, offering him better access. "Mark me, Malak."

He releases another tortured groan and then rolls us back onto our sides. He rests his forehead gently to my own, clenching his jaw. "If I mark you, my inner wolf will want to claim you," he whispers.

"But I'm already yours."

"You do not understand." His eyes snap to mine, dark with hunger. "It is instinct." A hint of a growl laces his words. "The wolf inside, and myself... we are one and the same. *My* desire for you is great, but *his* is ravenous. If I mark you now, he will not settle until we fully seal our bond."

Heat flushes my entire body as the understanding of what he means falls into place.

Breathless and panting, I can feel his heart pounding against my own. I want him. Desperately. But I'm worried it will be painful. "Will it hurt?" I whisper.

He freezes in place, and then lifts his head. His nostrils flare as he scents the wind. Without warning, he jumps to his feet and turns his back to me.

Panic grips me, and I quickly push myself up to standing. "What is it?"

Crouched in a defensive stance, his claws extend as he stares out at the darkness and a low and menacing growl rises in his throat. "Stay behind me. Someone is coming."

Ice freezes my veins as three sets of glowing eyes blink at us from the darkness. "Looks like you've saved us the trouble and caught this one already," someone says darkly.

"Why are you here?" Malak snarls.

A Wolf-Shifter with yellow eyes steps into view, followed

by another, their fangs bared, glinting beneath the silver moonlight as they approach. "The king has ordered the arrest of Ambassador Falen and his family," he grits out.

"Why would he do this?" Malak frowns.

"Avalor has declared war upon Winterhold. They sent a Mage to try to assassinate the royal family. Fortunately, he was killed." He narrows his eyes at me. "This assassin, however, was seen leaving Ambassador Falen's home this morning, and the king wants him to answer for these crimes."

Righteous anger burns in my chest. "My Father had nothing to do with—"

"Silence!" the closest one shouts. "Or I'll—"

"You *will not* touch her," Malak snarls, placing himself directly between them and me. "I am your prince, and I order you to stand down."

"We answer to your father," the second one sneers. "Not you. Now, step away from her, Prince Malak."

"No," Mal states firmly. "I will not."

"Your father has ordered the arrest of her and her family, and we will not leave here without her."

"Run, Luna," Mal whispers urgently. "Go. Now."

They shift into their four-legged wolven forms, and Malak quickly does the same. His black fur bristles in anger, and he releases a low and menacing growl as they stalk toward us, lips pulled back in feral snarls.

The closest one charges at me, but Malak blocks his path, colliding in a clash of fangs and claws as they twist and roll on the ground.

Blood stains the snow as they fight, locked together in a deadly embrace before Malak swipes his massive paw across his throat, slicing it open with his dagger-sharp claws.

The other two attack, launching themselves at Malak from either side. He rolls on the ground to shake them off, but one of them charges forward, sinking its fangs into his shoulder.

I know Mal wants me to run, but I cannot. I love him, and my love for him is stronger than my fear. I won't leave him behind.

Scanning the ground, I notice a fallen limb. I grip it firmly and rush toward the fight. Raising it overhead, I bring it down with all my strength, hitting one of the wolves with a sharp crack to his head.

He stumbles forward, and I take advantage of his imbalance to plunge my dagger into his back. He falls still and slumps to the side.

The third one raises its head and then pushes away from Malak to charge me.

Malak lunges for him, stopping him in his tracks. He clamps his massive jaws around his neck and rips his throat out. Blood sprays out as he collapses to the forest floor in a crumpled heap.

I force myself to look away from the bloodied scene, and Malak shifts back into his two-legged form. He gathers me in his arms, staring down at me with a panicked expression as he runs his hands over my body, checking for injury. "Are you hurt?"

Still in shock, my heart thunders as I reach a trembling hand to his bloodied chest. "You're bleeding, Mal."

"I'm fine," he says. "I am a Wolf-Shifter. We heal quickly. I will be all right."

Fear spikes through me, and I whip my head in the direction of the house. "My family."

Lightning fast, Malak hoists me into his arms and races through the forest with his inhuman speed.

When we reach the entryway, my mother rushes to us. "Thank the gods!" She blinks several times as she looks at Malak, covered in blood. "What happened?"

"We were attacked by the king's guards," I tell her. "Malak killed them, but—"

"We just received word," Mother says. "They said an assassin from Avalor tried to murder the royal family. A Mage. The king wants blood. Your father went to find you. We have to leave before—"

"Luna!" Father's voice calls out from behind us.

Malak spins with me still in his arms and my father's eyes widen as he takes in our bloodied appearance. He jumps down from his horse and rushes toward us.

"My father sent three guards to arrest you," Malak says as he carefully sets my feet back on the ground. "You need to take your family and leave. Now. But first, you must change into servant's clothing. Hurry."

"Why does the king think you're responsible, Father?" I ask, halting everyone in their tracks. "The king's guards said that you were seen with the assassin this morning."

Father jaw tightens. "He came to the house, but I knew not what he was planning."

Malak growls low in his chest, and my father goes silent, as he grinds out. "Do not speak unless the next words out of your mouth are truth, Ambassador Falen. And if you cannot do that, then at least do as I tell you from this point on if you want to save your family."

All the color drains from Father's face, and I stare in shock at Mal's harsh words. Father nods and then grabs Mother's hand, leading her back to the house.

Dozens of questions swirl through my mind as Malak and I follow behind them, but try as I might, I cannot speak around the lump of nerves in my throat. One of the servants brings us clothing to change into.

When we reach my room, Malak shuts the door behind us. Numbly, I move to the dressing partition to change. "Tell me," I force the words past my lips. "What has my father done?" Fully dressed in servant's clothing, I step back out into the room and face him. "What do you know about him that I do not?"

Mal shakes his head. "I was not certain that I was right until I accused your father of not telling the truth and saw his reaction. I observed him speaking with a man I did not recognize—a Mage—in the estate gardens this morning."

My heart slams in my throat. "What did they say?"

"Enough that I now know your father knew of his plans. He did not agree with them, but he did nothing to stop them either."

I place my hand over my heart as if that will dull the sharp stab of my father's betrayal. He knew an assassin was targeting the royal family. Mal is brother to the Crown Prince, and he is next in line for the throne if his brother were dead. "You would have been murdered too." The words leave my lips unfiltered as shock and anger flood my veins like ice. "Father would have—" My breath hitches, unable to continue.

"The assassin is dead, and my family still lives." Malak takes both my hands in his. "All that matters now is getting you to safety."

Worry fills me, but I force it back down as I struggle to formulate a plan. "I—I'm sure we can get you some papers when we reach Avalor. You can live under a different name until—"

"I'm not going."

My heart stutters and stops. "What?"

CHAPTER 7

MALAK

"No." Luna stares up at me in disbelief. "You have to come with us. You cannot stay here, Mal."

"I have to."

"You killed three of your father's guards. He will—"

"Do not worry about me, Luna." I cup her cheek. "You have to get to Avalor."

"You cannot stay here," she protests. "If he finds out you helped us escape, he'll—"

"He won't find out," I state firmly. "But if I leave with you, he will know. My father will send hunters to find me, and that will put you and your entire family in danger." I shake my head. "And I won't let that happen."

"Mal, please," she pleads. "You cannot stay here. It's too dangerous."

"How will we make it across the border?" I hear Luna's mother ask her father down the hallway. "Surely, they will be looking for us."

I turn back to Luna. "You probably only have half a day

before word spreads throughout the kingdom." My gaze drifts to her neck. "I need to give you my mark. If you are stopped at the border, show it to the guards. They will know you are a Wolf-Shifter's mate, and they will let you and your family through."

To my surprise, she turns her head and bares her neck to me. A growl rumbles in my chest at her complete trust and acceptance, my inner wolf clawing his way to the surface, desperate to claim our mate.

"I give you my most solemn vow." I cup her chin and stare deep into her lovely brown eyes. "You are mine, and I am yours. I will take no other as my mate."

"You are mine," she whispers in reply. "And I am yours. I will take no other as my mate."

Threading my fingers through her long red hair, I grip the silken strands and tilt her head to one side. My gaze locks on to the artery pulsing along the elegant curve of her neck.

She gasps as I clamp down with my fangs, clinging tightly to me as I apply just enough pressure to break through the delicate flesh.

Mine. My inner wolf growls as I leave my mark on her petal-soft skin. Everything inside me wants to hold her tight and never let her go. To claim her completely: mind, body, heart, and soul. But as much as I long to claim her in all ways, I cannot.

Not yet. She must go to Avalor, where she will be safe.

Blood pools at the bite mark, but I lave my tongue across the skin to stop the bleeding and start the healing process. It should be scarred over before they reach the border.

"You are my heart," I whisper, pressing a soft kiss to her neck, directly over my mark.

"Come with us, Mal." She wraps her arms around me, holding me close. "Please."

"I cannot. I have to speak with my father… make him see reason."

Luna's eyes are bright with tears. Cupping her face in both hands, I brush away the stray ones that run down her cheek. "If I leave with you now, he will hunt us. This is the only way you and your family will be safe."

"No." She shakes her head. "There must be another way."

"I will come to you, Luna," I promise. "I will find you again when it is safe. My vow."

I capture her mouth in a claiming kiss, tasting the salt of her tears as I try to hold back my own. I crush her to my chest, savoring this moment because I know it will be a long time before I will have her in my arms again.

Taking her hand in mine, I guide her down the stairs to her family. Her father curses as he struggles to loosen the straps holding the last horse to the carriage lead. I move to his side and unfasten it.

"Why are you helping me?" he asks, his voice low enough that I'm certain no one else heard him.

"I'm not helping *you*," I growl. "I'm saving my mate."

"*Mate?*" His head jerks back, eyes wide in shock. "Did you—"

"She is mine," I snarl. "I have given her my mark, and I will come for her when it is safe."

He shakes his head. "Your father will kill you if he finds out that you helped us. And he will never accept her. Not after what I have—"

"He will *not* find out," I grit through my teeth. "I've no doubt that this war your people have started will come to a bloody and vicious end soon. Each one of our warriors is worth a dozen of yours." I seethe.

I turn to face him fully, smelling his fear despite his otherwise stoic features. All the time spent among my people should have taught him that my kind can easily see through such facades. Scent never lies. "You were a fool not to warn my father when you could have. It would have saved the lives of thousands of your people."

"I want you to know that I did not condone the assassination attempt on your family."

"And yet you did *nothing* to stop it," I growl. "Your silence does not absolve you of your guilt, Ambassador Falen. My father *will* hold you responsible. And he will continue to do so, unless I can convince him otherwise."

"And what if you cannot?" The acrid scent of his fear grows stronger. "What then?"

My gaze shifts to Luna, standing with her mother near the other horses. I clench my jaw. "Your king was a fool to provoke my father. Do your best to convince him to beg forgiveness and mercy. War with Winterhold will only end in his ruin. Your kingdom cannot stand against mine and expect to win." He opens his mouth as if to protest, but I meet his gaze evenly. "Swallow your pride. You know I am right." I hand him the reins to the horse. "I will do my best to convince my father that peace is the answer. Avoid the main roads until you reach the border."

Without waiting for him to answer, I walk over to Luna while her father goes to her mother.

"Please," Luna pleads, her voice quavering softly. "Come with us, Mal."

I pull her into my arms, savoring her nearness. "You know I cannot."

"When will I see you again?"

"I will come for you when it is safe."

"Promise me." She blinks back tears. "Give me your vow."

"I have already given it." I trace my fingers over my mark on her neck, noting it is already healing. "You are my mate. I will come for you. My vow."

She stretches up on her toes and presses her lips to mine.

Wrapping my arms around her, I crush her to my chest as I deepen our kiss, trying to convey to her that she is all. She is everything. There will be no other for me. Now or ever. It is her and only her. And I will die before I break my promise.

When we finally pull away, I grip her waist and lift her up onto her horse. Her weight is so slight, it makes me afraid, worried thinking of how easily she could be hurt. My inner wolf claws and thrashes beneath the surface, fighting my resolve to send her away, insisting she is safer at our side.

Curling my hands into my fists, I force this dark and primal part of me to submit to my will. I do not make this decision lightly.

My heart is heavy as I watch Luna and her family ride away into the forest. Once they are gone, I force myself to focus on my task. I must make it appear as though Luna and her family are dead, buying them time to reach the border and get to safety.

I trek back into the woods and retrieve the fallen bodies of the guards, dragging them inside the main house. I pull a log from the burning hearth and over to the window. The curtains catch fire immediately, and I watch for a moment to make sure the flames spread.

As I walk away from the house, I shift back into wolf form and break into a run. The sooner I can convince my father that Luna's family had nothing to do with the attempt on my family's life, the sooner she will be in my arms again.

CHAPTER 8

LUNA

T*hree years later...*

THE CRUNCH of gravel draws my attention to the window as several carriages pull up outside the estate. The door to my room opens and my grandmother walks over to stand behind me, studying my reflection in the mirror. She adds a pearl comb to her graying, brown hair and then hands me a matching one for mine.

I smooth a hand over the silken skirt of my gown. Grandmother had this made for me, and it is stunning. The green is a beautiful contrast to my hair and eyes, but the bodice is so tight I can barely breathe.

The color and design are similar to the gown my grandmother wears. She instructed the seamstress to make sure the dresses complemented each other. The sigil of our House is embedded along the hem in golden thread, reminding everyone that we are related to the king.

"You are absolutely lovely, my darling granddaughter," she says, smiling as she rests her hands on my shoulders. "You remind me so much of your mother." Sadness flashes behind her brown eyes. "Your parents would be so proud to see the woman you've become."

I swallow against the lump rising in my throat. It has been two years since my parents passed. Father died fighting in the war, and Mother succumbed to the plague that ravaged the city shortly after. I miss them terribly.

"I've received word that the prince will make an offer for your hand before the evening is through," Grandmother says, and I force a smile to my face because I know it is what she expects by giving me this news.

My potential proposal to the prince is the culmination of months of negotiation between my grandmother and the king. After the war, and the death of the former monarch, King Brenor and his son, the crown is in need of money and legitimacy, both of which can be provided if the prince and I were to marry.

King Branac—the new king—is a distant cousin to the former one, leaving many to question his inheritance of the crown. His son—Prince Duren—and I share a great-great grandfather, who was once king of Avalor. Our marriage would create the illusion of an unbroken line, cementing their right to the throne.

My grandmother had my surname officially changed to match hers after my parents died, strengthening our family connection to the ancient line of kings. Her wealth survived the war intact, and she has made certain the king and the prince are aware of the healthy dowry they would receive if the prince took my hand.

I know she only wants what is best for me, but I am not

eager to marry the prince. We barely know each other, and many unflattering rumors surround him, including ones that suggest he may find it hard to remain faithful to our marriage bed.

My hair is braided with green ribbon and twisted atop my head like a crown. My eyes travel over the mark on my neck. It is so faint, it is easy for most to overlook, but not me. Each time I wear my hair up, I think of Malak, remembering the last time I saw him.

A dull ache settles deep in my chest as I reach up and trace my fingers over the light scarring. I thought it was a promise, but I was wrong.

Not long after we returned to Avalor, Malak sent me a message. He told me we could not be together and that I should forget about him. A few months later, I received word he was betrothed to Lady Rysa, daughter of the Wolf Shifter leader of Ilanthos, uniting the Southern pack with that of his family's.

Grandmother's gaze tracks my hand, and she shakes her head softly. "Oh, Luna," she gently chastises. "It has been three years. You must let him go, my dear."

"I have, Grandmother." At least… that's what I keep telling myself even as I tuck the necklace with the golden ring he gave me under the collar of my dress. "Truly."

At first, I'd thought the letter was a lie, because it had nothing of our code in it. But when I finally heard news that he was engaged, it shattered my heart. It took a long time to piece it back together, but I finally have. And now… it is time to move on.

"Prince Duren just arrived, and he has already inquired about you." She grins. "I told him you would be down short- ly." Her gaze shifts to the window. "It seems nearly everyone is here."

As I study my grandmother's reflection in the mirror, I

can't help but think she is more excited about this ball than me. She's been planning this for months. All with the intent of enticing the prince to attend and ask for my hand. It appears that all her negotiations and planning will finally come to fruition this night.

The couple of times we have spoken, Prince Duren seemed to be an amiable person, and we do have a few things in common, but there is no… spark, for lack of a better word. At least, not on my part. Grandmother insists it does not matter. All that's important is that we get along. Which we do.

Of course, all her planning could be for nothing. I am not the only eligible woman that will be in attendance tonight. Nor will the prince be the only unmarried man at this ball. Lords and Ladies from all corners of the kingdom and some even beyond its borders will be here this evening, many of them hoping to find an advantageous match.

A knock at the door brings forth one of the servants. She enters with a huge bouquet of pink roses. A beaming smile lights her face as she sets them in the vase on the table beside me. "The prince said I should bring these up to you right away, Lady Luna."

Grandmother clasps her hands together and then kisses the top of my head. "He's going to ask for your hand this evening, I just know it."

When she first suggested a match between me and the prince, I thought her mad. There are many eligible ladies of the court who come from wealthy families. Most of them are exceptionally beautiful, and a few have even been rumored to catch Prince Duren's eye.

None of them but me, however, have the pedigree the prince and his father need to secure their power. And, judging from the gift of flowers, it would seem Prince Duren has made his choice.

Grandmother grabs the powder from the stand and dabs some more over the mark on my neck, scowling until it is completely hidden beneath the makeup. She grins. "There. Much better."

I know she is only trying to be helpful, but every time any attention is drawn to my mark, my heart feels heavy all over again.

"Are you ready, my dear?" she asks as she hands me my mask.

The intricate white and gold pattern is lovely, but I frown when I notice the elongated ears on either side. "A hare?" It's bad enough that this event makes me feel like I'm about to be prey in the midst of several predators. "Is there nothing else?"

She holds out her own mask. "Would you prefer a cat?"

I shake my head, don my mask, and then follow her downstairs.

The entire estate has been decorated for the masquerade ball. Grandmother spared no expense. My gaze travels over the glittering silk ribbons that wind down the banister and around the columns, golden vases overflowing with vibrant flowering arrangements, and tables heavily laden with food and drink.

Golden chandeliers hang from the ceiling in the ballroom, their candlelight reflecting off the ceiling and the walls, casting beautiful patterns across the floor. A string quartet plays in the corner, as men dressed in their finery and women in gorgeous dresses dance to the lovely music. At least two dozen couples, each of them wearing masks, spin and whirl across the floor in almost perfect synchrony with each other.

I grab a goblet and sip at my wine, hoping it will steady my nerves. As much as I want to please my grandmother, I'm not entirely sure how I will react if Prince Duren truly does ask for my hand this evening. He was kind to me when we spoke, and we have a few common interests, but is that enough for a successful marriage? Or should there be more?

Just as I'm beginning to wonder if anyone can tell who is who beneath their mask, I notice Prince Duren speaking with my grandmother across the room.

When they are finished, he walks over to me. His bright blue eyes are a sharp contrast to his golden mask with antlers. His mask was no doubt chosen to represent the royal sigil of their House—the Stag.

He smooths a hand through his short, blond curls and then dips his chin in greeting. "Lady Luna"—he offers his hand with a subtle bow—"may I have this dance?"

"Yes," I reply, offering him my best attempt at a smile.

He takes my hand and guides me onto the floor. His skin is soft, but then again, he is the Crown Prince of Avalor, and I suppose, like his father, he does not train with their guards, and any sort of labor is beneath him.

He's taller than me, though not by much, and when I grip his shoulder with my free hand, I'm surprised by how much padding seems to be incorporated into his tunic, for I cannot feel anything of his actual shoulder.

Duren puts his free hand on my waist and then leads me in a waltz. His steps are sure and graceful. It is well-known the prince loves to dance. He smiles at me as we spin and whirl across the floor, and I'm acutely aware of all the eyes trained in our direction.

His hand slides from my waist to my back and he pulls me closer. My heart races knowing that our position is on the razor's edge of propriety and, although he is the prince and may soon be my betrothed, I will not allow him to take any liberties with me.

Gently, I push away, putting some space between us, and his grin widens. "That's why I like you, Luna," he says, his gaze sweeping over the room. "I'm sure most of the other women here would have made to move closer to me simply because of who I am, regardless of how it may look to others. But you challenge me, and I do enjoy a challenge."

His sharp eyes pin me with an assessing and uncomfortable stare. "I had a horse once, that was stubborn. A beautiful chestnut mare." He sighs wistfully. "No one could break her. It took me two years, but I finally did."

I'm not quite sure what to make of his statement other than that I find it deeply unsettling.

He continues. "Do not worry about propriety this night." He leans in and whispers. "I have already asked your grandmother for your hand, and she has agreed. You are mine, and we may do whatever we wish."

Dread slithers down my spine as his eyes travel up and down my form meaningfully. Steeling myself, I tip up my chin. "You asked my grandmother, but you have not yet asked me."

He frowns. "Are you suggesting you would deny my offer?"

"I—" I stop short as something catches my eye over his shoulder. A man in a black and gold wolf's mask. He is tall and his shoulders are broad. Dressed in a green that matches my dress, with black pants and boots, his outfit does little to hide his heavily muscled form beneath. He moves through the crowd with the preternatural grace of a predator. He has short, dark hair and as his piercing green eyes meet mine, I inhale sharply at the flash of recognition.

Malak.

"No," I whisper, more to myself than to anyone else.

"No?" Duren asks incredulously. "What on earth are you saying?"

"Not you," I say quickly, turning my attention back to him. "What I mean is, I was speaking of something else."

He gives me a quizzical look. "Something… else?"

I glance back over his shoulder, but the man is gone. Frantically, I scan the crowd, wondering if I'm going mad. Or perhaps it's the drink already affecting me. I've never had a high tolerance for wine or mead.

"Luna?" Prince Duren says, pulling my attention back to his frowning features. "Are you all right?"

Maybe it's that my bodice is too tight and it's making me delusional. "I—I think I need to get some fresh air."

He nods and starts to guide me outside, but I stop him. "I'll only be a moment." I offer him a placating smile. "You should enjoy yourself, Prince Duren. I know how much you love dancing."

A wide grin spreads across his face, and he kisses my hand. "Do not worry." He winks. "It is you I will be thinking of when I am dancing."

I plaster another smile on my face and then watch in relief as he slips back out onto the floor. In less than a second, he already has another partner. A woman with golden hair that matches his and a bright red dress with a neckline that seems far too revealing to be proper.

Turning away, I push open the doors and step outside into the gardens. I tug at my bodice, trying to loosen it a bit as I draw in several breaths. None of them are deep, however, no thanks to this suffocating torture device of a bodice and the corset beneath. I growl in frustration as I try to loosen it again to no avail.

Movement catches the corner of my eye, and I still. The hairs rise on the back of my neck as I lift my head and scan the garden. Something is watching me, but I do not know what or who.

Glowing green eyes blink at me from the darkness, and my mouth drops as a dark wolf comes into focus.

Much larger than a regular wolf, I'm certain it is a shifter.

My heart stops. Wolf-Shifters are not supposed to be in Avalor. It was one of the accords agreed to when they signed the treaty with Winterhold at the end of the war.

And while I am aware that there are many Wolf-Shifters with black fur, I cannot ignore the part of me that wonders if it could be Mal.

Without thinking, I start toward it, but it turns and heads for the back gate. "Wait!"

It glances briefly over its shoulder but keeps walking to the forest beyond the garden wall.

"Wait!" I call out again, and it slows. "Are you—" The words get stuck in my throat, and I cannot speak as my heart hammers.

Gathering my skirts, I pick up my pace and head down the garden path toward the wolf.

My pulse pounds in my ears, and I struggle to breathe as I hurry. My corset feels as if it's digging into my ribs, constricting my lungs with each hurried step, but I cannot stop as I keep my gaze fixed on the wolf.

"Malak?" I somehow force the word past my lips. "Is that you?"

The wolf turns and sprints into the woods, and before I even realize what I'm doing, I'm chasing after it. "Wait!"

This is dangerous—foolish to run off into the woods after some strange wolf that may or may not be who I think he is. I've heard stories of maidens who were lured by trickster Fae into the forests, that could alter their shape, and despite the warnings sounding in my head, my heart urges me to pursue.

It's Malak. It has to be. I don't know how I know this for sure, but I trust my instincts.

I only pray they are right. I do not want to end up as a cautionary tale about women running off into the woods and being taken by some devious Otherworldly being with bad intent.

Racing out into the forest, my body struggles to drag in each labored breath. "This blasted corset," I curse as I push through the woods, each step more dizzying than the last.

The wolf is just up ahead, and I fear I cannot go any further without passing out. "Wait!" I cry out. "I cannot keep running like this." I wheeze, bracing myself on a nearby tree trunk as my chest heaves with each ragged breath.

With my free hand, I try to reach back to loosen the knot of my corset, but the movement only makes everything feel even tighter than before. The world spins around me, and I stumble forward.

Strong arms catch me around the waist, and I blink up at a shadowy figure leaning over me.

"Luna." My heart squeezes painfully in my chest at the familiar deep tone of Malak's voice. Moonlight spears through the branches, illuminating his face in silver light.

He is even more handsome than I remembered.

My head is spinning, and I don't know if this is real or not. With a trembling hand, I touch his face. "Is this a dream?" I barely manage.

"What is wrong?" His green eyes stare down at me in concern.

"My corset is too tight," I force the words past my lips. "It's constricting my—"

The sound of ripping fabric fills the air as Malak slices the ribbon of my corset with his sharp claws. I draw in several deep, gulping breaths.

"Better?" he asks.

I nod, but confusion quickly overshadows my relief. "What are you doing here?"

"I came for you," he says. "Just as I vowed that I would."

I thought nothing could ever hurt me as much as his letter, but as he stands before me now, saying the words I dreamed of him saying so many times, my heart shatters all over again. Tears sting my eyes, as my hurt wars with anger. I push at his chest, to put some space between us. His strong hands are still wrapped around my waist as if to steady me, but I bat them away and take a step back.

"Luna, what is wrong?"

"What's wrong?" I ask incredulously. "You told me to forget about you, Malak. And the last I heard you were engaged to someone else." I gesture to him. "So, what are you doing here now? Why have you come?"

A traitorous tear slips down my cheek, but I quickly brush it away. I do not want to cry in front of him. Not now. "Why after all this time, Mal?"

His brow furrows deeply. "Because you are mine, Luna."

Pain spears through me. A sob rises in my throat, but I swallow it back down, not wanting to appear pitiful or weak. He broke my heart, and now he has the audacity to claim that he still wants me?

My corset starts to fall from my body, and my sadness is quickly replaced by raw anger. If anyone sees me like this, there will be a scandal for sure. My reputation will be ruined, as will any prospect of a respectable future.

Malak hurt me before, and I will *not* let him ruin me.

His eyes snag on my necklace and the ring he gave me, hanging on the end, but he says nothing.

Glaring at Malak, I hold my corset to my chest and bite my bottom lip to stop it from quivering. "I am not yours." I struggle to keep my voice even despite my pain and anger. "You *chose* someone else. You made it very clear that you didn't want me, Malak. So, do *not* come here claiming that I am yours, because *you* cast *me* aside, remember?"

CHAPTER 9

MALAK

Luna's anger is a blade in my heart. I never stopped wanting her, but I could not allow my father to think that I did. "I lied to protect you," I explain. "I had to. My father would have sent assassins to finish what his guards did not, if he knew what I felt for you. "Please, Luna, I—"

I stop as my gaze drops to the elegant curve of her neck. Devastation fills me. She has covered my mark with a thick layer of makeup, so that it is barely visible. How could she do such a thing? Marking is sacred—a sign of the unbreakable bond between mates.

"You covered my mark." My nostrils flare at the betrayal. "And you were dancing with another male."

"Why do you care?" Anger burns in her eyes. "You are betrothed to another. Or was that a lie too?"

"No," I reply, and she recoils as if struck. "My father arranged our engagement to unite our two packs. He needed them for the war against your people."

"Where is your betrothed now, Malak? Does she know you have come? Did you give her your mark and a promise you've no intention to keep?" she asks accusingly. "Like you did to me?"

"No." Her words are sharp barbs in my heart. "A wolf only marks one person in their entire life. I told her that I could not bond with her. That I still—"

"Stop!" She holds out her hand. "I do not want to hear it."

"You are my mate, Luna." I clench my jaw. "We swore a vow to each other."

"I don't belong to you, Malak. You *left* me. Or have you forgotten?"

"I had to. It was the only way to keep you safe." I shake my head. "But I'm here now."

"Three years too late," she snaps.

Jealousy churns deep within as the smell of the other male on her skin and clothing is carried toward me on the cool breeze. "Who was that male you were dancing with?"

"Prince Duren of Avalor," she replies. "We are to be betrothed this night."

A low growl rises in my chest as my inner wolf claws beneath the surface, demanding that we end this male who dares think he can claim her.

She is *my* mate. *Not* his.

"You pledged yourself to me," I remind her. "We swore vows to each other."

"*You* told me to forget you, Malak. You told me to move on, and I did." She throws the words of my letter back at me, like daggers straight to my heart. "And now you show up, and lure me into the woods..." She bites her bottom lip to stop it from quivering and turns her back to me.

"You cannot marry another, Luna," I plead. "You are my mate. You carry my mark, and I am yours."

Her back is still turned to me as I step closer. So close that the warmth of her body radiates to mine. Gently, I dip my head to the elegant curve of her neck and scent her, as I used to do so often.

"Please don't," her voice quavers, and I can smell the salt of her tears. She steps away from me and straightens, tipping up her chin. "I have to get back."

"Luna, please, we must talk."

"Not out here," she says, her voice devoid of emotion. She glances down at her loosened bodice. "I need to get back. I—" Her voice catches. "I cannot be seen like this."

"Why?"

"I need to sneak back to my room and change. Something like this—" she gestures to her torn bodice—"could so easily be misconstrued, and then I would be ruined and my grand-mother would be shamed."

"Humans and their strange proprieties," I grumble.

"Perhaps they are strange to you," she says icily, "but I have had to live with them for the past three years."

I open my mouth to ask, but she pins me with a hard gaze. "We were at war with your people, and I carried your mark. The mark of a wolf's mate. You have no idea what it was like. I—" Her voice catches, and she swallows hard before continuing. "Everyone overlooks it now because with my hand comes a handsome dowry from my grandmother. Even the royal family of Avalor would ignore it to restore their fortune and keep their throne."

With one hand holding her bodice to her chest, she grips the skirt of her dress with the other and starts back toward the house.

"Luna, wait," I call out. "We need to talk."

She casts an angry glare over her shoulder before she pushes through the back gate, but I take comfort in knowing that she still carries my ring on her necklace. Surely, it means she still has feelings for me... that she still loves me as I love her.

A sharp cry rings out, startling us both. Lightning fast, I pull Luna behind me, and my eyes widen when I see her betrothed with another female.

The woman gasps as she pushes to her feet. Her red dress is halfway down her body as she rushes away, trying desperately to fit her arms back in the sleeves.

Struggling to pull his pants back up his legs, Luna's betrothed trips and falls forward in the grass. His jaw drops as Luna steps out from behind me.

"This—this isn't what it looks like," he says. "I—I swear."

"This night just keeps getting better," Luna murmurs under her breath, her tone laced with sarcasm.

"Oh, really?" I tell him. Tipping my face up, I sniff the air and wrinkle my nose. "Because this looks and smells like a mating," I spit out in disgust. His scent is an assault on my senses. He smells like several days of poor hygiene, pitifully masked with cologne and alcohol. "You reek of filth, human."

Although I am glad to see he has already proven how worthless he is, I am angry that he would have even dared to touch Luna, much less ask for her hand.

"How dare you speak to me like this." He scowls. "I am the Prince of Avalor."

"Regardless of titles, you are still a pig," I snarl.

His head jerks back, and his shocked expression morphs into anger. "And what of you two?" He gestures animatedly at Luna, holding her bodice to her chest. "What were *you* both doing out in the woods?"

Instead of trying to justify herself, Luna narrows her eyes as she points an accusing finger at him. "Mention anything of this, and I'll tell everyone of your exploits as well."

Without waiting for him to respond, she runs toward the side of the house, and I follow closely behind her. Thick vines trail up the outer wall to a balcony overhead. She turns to me. "Help me get up."

In one smooth motion, I lift her into my arms. She squeaks in surprise as I put her over my shoulder, and then climb up the vines to the balcony above. When we reach the top, I carefully set her back on her feet, and we slip through the door into what I assume is her room.

She turns to me, pursing her lips. "I didn't need you to carry me. I just needed a little help to get started, but I could have climbed up myself, you know."

Her bodice starts to slip off again before she presses it to her chest. I arch a brow, and she huffs out an irritated breath as she rolls her eyes.

She walks to her wardrobe, searching for something else to wear.

Frustration burns through me as she acts as if I'm not even here. "That's it? You have nothing else to say?"

"I'm thinking," she says icily.

I walk up behind her and gently slip my arms around her waist. "Luna, please. Forgive me."

"Don't you dare touch me," she hisses, pushing me away. "You have no idea what your letter did to me." Her voice breaks on the last word. "I—"

A sharp knock at the door startles us both, followed by a woman's voice. "Luna, are you in there?"

"One minute, Grandmother," she calls out. "I'll be right there."

She turns to me, urgency in her features. "You need to hide."

"What?"

"Now," she states firmly.

"Why?"

"Because, as I stated before, we are in Avalor, not Winterhold. And *here*, it is improper for me to be alone with a man."

"I'm not a man, I'm a Wolf-Shifter," I correct. "And not just any Wolf-Shifter, I am your mate. There is nothing improper about my being here with—"

She grips my wrist and tugs me to the wardrobe. "Hide." With a strength I did not know she possessed, Luna pushes me inside and slams it shut. "Stay quiet, Mal." She eyes me through the narrow gap between the doors. "I mean it."

She pulls off her bodice and gown, leaving her only in her shift. Pulling a heavy robe around her shoulders, she answers the door.

Her grandmother pushes inside. Following on her heels is Prince Duren.

I bite back a growl as the prince turns toward her grandmother. "If you do not mind, I'd like a moment alone with my intended." Indecision plays out across the elder woman's features before he adds. "I know it may be a bit improper for us to be alone, but you will be right outside the door to dispel any vicious rumors for us."

She nods and steps back out into the hallway.

As soon as the door shuts behind her, Luna places her hands on her hips, narrowing her eyes. "Why are you here?"

"I—" Shock is easily read in his features. As a prince, he is probably unused to anyone speaking to him in such a manner. He narrows his eyes as he walks toward her. "Do you not realize who it is you are speaking to? I am your prince and future husband, and I will not be treated this way."

She curls her hands into fists at her sides, leveling an angry glare at him. She opens her mouth to speak, but he interrupts.

"Remember what I told you about my chestnut mare?" He stalks closer. "If I have to throw you in the castle dungeons to break you, I will."

All the color drains from Luna's face, and unbridled rage

blisters through me. Without hesitation, I burst out of the wardrobe and pull Luna behind me, placing myself between her and the prince, baring my fangs. "You *will not* threaten my mate."

Duren's jaw drops.

"If you dare touch her," I growl. "I will rip your head from your shoulders."

His shock quickly turns to anger. "You are the one who left that unseemly mark on her neck," he sneers. "Tell me: what is your name, Wolf? And do you not realize that your presence here violates our treaty, the penalty of which is immediate execution?"

I straighten, glaring down at him in contempt. "I am Prince Malak of Winterhold, and High Lord of the Vale," I grind out. "Threaten me, and you will have a war on your hands that you know you will not win."

"Guards!" he calls out and two men and a woman burst through the door.

My eyes widen as a glowing red orb hovers between the woman's palms.

A low growl rips from my throat. She is a Mage, and while others would cower, I am not afraid. Avalor employed several of them during the war, and I have dealt with her kind before.

With a flick of her wrists, she sends an arc of magic flying toward me.

"No!" Luna cries out, a moment before it slams against the invisible, protective barrier that surrounds me thanks to the protective rune carved on my back.

The Mage's sinister expression falls.

I narrow my eyes. "My kind learned very quickly how to combat your dark powers."

Before she can respond, I lunge forward to attack.

She spins away, casting another orb toward Luna. It slams

against the invisible barrier around her, exploding in a brilliant burst of light. Her jaw drops.

"She is my mate," I growl. "Your powers cannot touch her."

"Stop this at once!" Luna's grandmother calls out, but a dozen more guards push past her through the door, each of them drawing their swords.

"Perhaps my magic cannot," the Mage says darkly. "But weapons certainly can."

Lightning fast, I transform into my wolven form. "Touch her and you die," I snarl. "My vow."

"Kill the wolf, but do not harm the girl," the prince commands. "Capture her! Now!"

This Mage is powerful, and while I believe I can best her, dozens of bootsteps echo on the stairs as more guards rush to the aid of their prince.

I cannot risk Luna being hurt, and I refuse to leave her in the clutches of Prince Duren. I must protect my mate.

Shifting back into my two-legged form, I hoist her to my chest and run outside onto the balcony. Without hesitation, I leap from the railing, and Luna cries out in surprise as we fly through the air before landing solidly on the ground below.

Without stopping, I race through the gardens toward the forest. If I can reach it before the Mage and the guards follow, we have a chance.

"After them!" Prince Duren's voice shouts from the balcony behind us. "Hunt them down! Bring me his head! Do whatever it takes to find them!"

"I'm going to shift," I tell her. "And I need you to ride on my back."

She nods. As soon as we push through the back gate, I set her down and then take a healthy step back. With a whirl of leaves and wind, I transform back into wolven form. Kneeling down, I urge Luna to climb on.

CHAPTER 10

LUNA

I've seen Malak shift into his wolven form before, but his sheer size never ceases to amaze me. He is much larger than a regular wolf, with thick, black fur, and glowing green eyes. He kneels and I quickly scramble onto his back, settling over his shoulders. I grip tightly to his heavy coat, and he lunges forward, racing through the forest.

The trees and the landscape blur around us and the wind claws at my body as he rushes through the woods at breakneck speed. He is fast in his two-legged form, but even more so in this one.

Panic spikes through me when I catch sight of a ravine up ahead. Instead of slowing like I'd expected, he picks up his speed. *"We're going to jump,"* his voice whispers in my mind. *"Hold tightly to me."*

Bracing myself, I squeeze my eyes shut and hold firmly to him. The powerful muscles of his body bunch beneath me a moment before he jumps, sailing through the air.

I nearly lose my grip on his fur when he lands on the other side, but I somehow manage to remain upright.

Only now that we've made it across do I realize that he spoke in my mind. "Did you—"

"It is our bond," he explains in my head. *"Mated pairs can speak in this way to one another when they are near each other in wolven form."*

"Can you hear me?" I think to him, testing the connection.

"Yes." He pauses. *"The bond also allows some mated pairs to sense each other's emotions."*

I'm not sure how I feel about him being privy to my innermost thoughts and emotions.

A rolling boom of thunder sounds overhead, interrupting my worried musings. Dark clouds blanket the sky, and a light mist of rain begins to fall.

"We need to find shelter," Malak says.

"There's an inn not far from here," I offer. "In the town of—"

"No," he replies sharply. *"The prince will expect us to go there. We must keep off the main roads until we are closer to the border."*

He continues on his path, taking us deeper into the woods.

The skies open up as rain begins to fall. My damp clothes stick to my skin and plaster my hair to my face and neck, chilling me straight to the bone. What I wouldn't give for a thick, winter cloak as the cold breeze picks up, weaving through the trees and wrapping around me in an icy embrace.

After what feels like forever, we finally find a rocky outcropping. It isn't much, but at least it's some sort of shelter from the freezing rain. Malak lowers himself to the ground, and I slide off his back. My teeth begin chattering, and I miss the warmth of his contact.

He shifts into his two-legged form and wraps his arms

around me. He pulls me into his lap as he sits down. Cold and tired, I curl into his embrace. Gently, he nuzzles the top of my head. The gesture so intimate and familiar, my chest tightens. "Is this better?" he whispers.

Swallowing against the knot of emotions in my throat, I nod.

How many times did I dream of him holding me like this? How many nights did I cry myself to sleep because I thought he did not care? Memories flood my mind, along with all the hurt and the pain I've felt these past few years. A sharp ache stabs at my chest and my heart shatters all over again as he holds me so tenderly in his arms. As if I am a rare and precious thing. I swallow back a sob. I don't want to cry. I've already shed too many tears.

"I missed you," he whispers into my hair. "So much. Did you—" He pauses a moment as if unsure what to say before finally managing, "think of me often?"

"Every day," I admit, my voice barely a whisper.

He cups my chin, brushing the pad of his thumb across my lower lip.

The intimacy of his touch is a blade in my heart. I cannot simply forget all the pain of these past few years.

His face falls as I pull away. "Luna, what is wrong?"

"How can you act as though nothing has changed, Malak?" Tears sting the back of my eyes.

"Because it hasn't." His gaze holds mine. "You are my mate, Luna."

"You say I'm your mate, but I thought Wolf-Shifters didn't abandon their mates," I reply sharply, unable to hide the anger in my tone. "Your letter, Malak... that's what you did. You left me."

"I had no choice, Luna."

"Yes, you did," I insist. "Do you have any idea what you

did to me?" A tear slips down my cheek. "You could have used our code… You could have explained—"

"I could not risk using the code and having my father discover my true feelings." He takes my hand. "But I came for you, Luna. I'm here now."

"What has changed?" I ask. "Why now?"

"I have been searching for you since my father's death," he says. "But I could not find you. I sent spies to track down any hint of your location, but it was as if you had disappeared entirely. My mother told me to prepare myself that you might be gone." He tightens his arms around me. "I feared you were dead." He frowns. "Why did you change your surname? Was it to hide from my father?"

"No."

"To hide from me, then?" he asks, his expression suddenly vulnerable as he waits for my answer.

I shake my head. "It was my grandmother's idea, after my parents died."

"I am sorry that you lost them, Luna," he says softly.

Emotions tighten my throat, but I force myself to speak around them. "Thank you. And I am sorry for what my father did to your family, Malak. Even if he did not directly —" My voice hitches, and it takes me a moment to continue. "His complicity was wrong. He should have warned your family. Even if it made him a traitor to his kingdom."

Malak remains silent a moment before he speaks. "Whatever his crimes, he loved you and your mother, Luna. Do not let what happened tarnish your memory of him."

Reluctantly, I nod. Closing my eyes, I force the painful memories to retreat before I continue, returning the subject back to his previous question. "You asked why my grandmother changed my surname. It is because my mother's family… their name can be traced back to the ancient line of kings. She did it to strengthen our status and secure a marriage to the crown prince. The new royal family needs my family's name and my grandmother's wealth to ensure that their claim to the throne remains unchallenged."

"Were you truly going to marry him?" Mal asks.

Sighing heavily, I lower my gaze. "I do not know."

"Do you love him?"

Frustration burns in my chest. "What does it matter?"

"It matters to *me*," he says, his voice laced with a growl.

Wolf-Shifters are extremely possessive and territorial, but Malak has no right to be angry. Not after he hurt me. "How dare you get angry," I lash out. "You're the one who told me to move on. You *left* me, Malak."

He remains silent a moment before he finally responds. "I am here now, Luna," he says softly. "Fredrik is king of Winterhold, and I am High Lord of the Vale, and I want you to be my High Lady."

Everything is happening so fast; none of it seems real. Less than an hour ago I was sure he had forgotten about me. But now he's here... asking me to be his High Lady. Instead of addressing his statement, I ask a question. "How did you get the Vale? I thought Trolls had taken it while Winterhold was distracted with the war."

"They did," he replies grimly. "I knew how badly my father wanted it back. So when the war ended, I made a bargain with him. If I reclaimed the Vale for Winterhold, it would be mine to rule, and as such, I could live my life as I chose... take whoever I wanted as my mate."

He takes my hand. "I did it for you, Luna. I knew I would eventually find you. And when I did, I needed somewhere we could live that would be safe. Away from my father... away from anyone or anything that would dare try to keep us apart."

I swallow against the lump in my throat as I look down at our joined hands. "You want everything to be as it was, but it's been three years, Malak," I fight to keep my voice even despite my pain. "I am not the same person I was when you left me."

"Yes, you are."

"No, I'm not," I counter. "The person I was"—I shake my head softly—"she cried herself to sleep so many nights thinking you'd forgotten her."

"But I did not forget you."

"How was I to know that? You hurt me, Malak. I was so devastated, and I—" My voice catches and tears track down my cheeks.

Cupping my face, he brushes them away, his gaze full of sadness. "Do you still love me?"

"It is not that simple." My heart has yearned for him all this time, but everything inside me is afraid. He has no idea the pain that he caused, and I don't know if I can trust him not to hurt me again.

"Yes, it is." He drops his forehead gently to mine. "My heart has always belonged to you. And if you will give me a chance, I will prove myself worthy of yours again." His green eyes stare deep into mine. "You are my mate, and I do not want anyone else but you. Please, do not push me away, Luna."

His words pierce my heart.

All this time, I thought I had gotten over him, but I know now that I was wrong. With just one look, he has already broken through the walls around my heart.

CHAPTER 11

MALAK

My heart clenches as I wait for her reply, worried she will reject me.

"I need time, Malak," she speaks softly.

I'm relieved at her answer. She still loves me. I know she must. If she did not, she would have said so. Instead, she has asked for time.

This is something I can give her. And in doing so, I vow that I will prove to her that I am worthy to be hers. That I can be the mate that she deserves.

"I understand."

Rain continues to fall around us, and an icy wind blows through the woods. I tighten my arms around her, and she nestles into me, still shivering. "This will not do," I whisper. "I need to shift forms."

I gently set her on the ground and step back. In a whirl of dust and leaves, I shift into my wolven form and then return to her side. I curl my body around hers, and she nestles against me. Draping my tail over her body, I am pleased when a soft sigh of contentment leaves her mouth. "Thank you, Mal."

I love the familiar way my name rolls off her tongue, reminding me of the days when she so freely loved me. Before I broke her heart.

"Do you remember that time we got caught out in the snow in the forest?" she asks.

I turn my head toward her, arching a brow. *"I recall that I told you the weather was turning, but you insisted that we stay out."*

"I thought it was only going to be a light snow," she says wistfully. "How was I to know it would turn into a blizzard?"

Playfully, I nudge her shoulder with my snout. *"Because I told you it would."*

"You and those superior wolf senses of yours." A faint smile curves her mouth. "My parents were so worried... They thought I was dead." She traces her hand along my jaw. "But you kept us safe and warm like this."

I lean into her palm, relishing the contact between us. When we were younger, before we'd admitted our feelings for each other, I would often take this form, knowing how much more comfortable she was... how easily she would touch me like this.

My inner wolf knew then that she was my fated mate long before I even recognized it myself.

She snuggles further into my side, and I drape my tail over her form to cover her. "What did you do after we left?" she asks. "How did you keep your father from coming after us?"

"I burned the estate to the ground, with my father's guards inside. I paid the servants to be quiet, and my father believed you and your family had died in the fire."

Her jaw drops.

"He did not even know I'd been gone from the capital when I

returned that night. He was so preoccupied with the failed assassi-nation attempt, that he was already planning his retaliation and the war against Avalor. Fredrik lied for me, claiming I had gone off somewhere because I was still mad at my father for refusing my decision to take you as my mate.

"And when he received word about the ruined estate, it was not hard for me to put on the appearance of grieving your loss." I meet her eyes evenly. *"I missed you."*

She lowers her gaze, and I continue. *"When he finally discovered you were still alive, it was too late. You and your family were already in Avalor."* I pause. *"What did you do after you escaped?"*

Her gaze drifts to the forest with a faraway look. "At first, Father sent me and Mother into hiding, worried your father would send assassins. When Winterhold pushed through our borders, your warriors were so close to the capital, we had to evacuate to the south. Father was favored by the king because of his knowledge of your kingdom, and so we were evacuated with the royal family and the upper nobility."

A low growl rumbles my chest as I think of Prince Duren. I'd always heard he was a rake and then witnessed it in the gardens. The thought of him touching Luna sends fire racing through my veins. *"Did you spend much time with the prince then?"*

"There were many people there, including him. But he was not the prince at that time," she points out.

I bite back a growl. I know I have no right to be upset or to even ask, but I cannot stop the words from leaving my mouth. *"How close were you to him?"*

Her eyes snap to mine, fire burning behind them. She is right to be angry with me. I was the one who pushed her away.

"Forgive me," I say quickly. Even if she has had dozens of

lovers, it would not matter. I love her and nothing will change that. *"I've no right to—"*

"There has been no one," she says in a voice so low I almost miss it. "You are the only one who has ever touched me."

Primal possessiveness unfurls from deep within as my inner wolf revels in her words. My gaze darts to my mark on her neck and the desire to claim her fully burns like fire in my veins. All these years, I have dreamed of the taste of her lips and the sweet salt of her skin and the delicious scent of her body as she responds to my touch.

But I must be patient. I hurt her, and I broke her trust. Now, I must find a way to earn it back and to win her heart once more. I will do whatever it takes to make her mine, for I will never want another as I desire her.

CHAPTER 12

LUNA

"I've missed you," his voice whispers in my mind. *"Every day since we parted."*

I've missed him too, but I cannot tell him this. The words remain buried under the bitter pain of these past few years. Even though I understand now why he wrote me the letter that broke my heart, and why he was engaged to someone else, the dull ache in my chest stubbornly remains.

He nuzzles my side with his long snout. *"What are you thinking?"* he whispers in my head.

Instead of answering, a bitter laugh leaves my lips. "I thought you could read my thoughts."

"I can pick up some things... wisps of emotion, but not everything."

"What can you sense now?" I ask, unable to hide the biting edge in my tone.

His green eyes search mine, sadness and guilt shining behind them. *"I hurt you."*

A tangle of emotions tightens around my heart, and I bite my bottom lip to stop it from quivering.

"Luna, everything I did was to protect you. I—"

"I don't want to speak of it right now, Mal." I force the words out of my mouth. "I'm tired. We're in the middle of the forest, in the rain, and possibly being chased by the prince." Exhaustion seeps into my bones. "I just—" I swallow against the lump in my throat. "I don't know what to do."

I shiver slightly, and his voice fills my mind. *"We will have to go to one of the towns. You need proper clothing or else you'll risk falling ill."*

"I need to get word to my grandmother. She is probably so worried for me, Mal," I add. "And we need to find a way to get you safely across the border. Your presence in Avalor violates the treaty. The prince and his father will declare war if—"

"If they do, both Winterhold and the Vale will beat them back," he states firmly. *"I would prefer not to go to war, but we did it before, and we will do it again if we must."* He meets my gaze evenly. *"I want you to come to the Vale with me. We can send for your grandmother once we're safely across the border."*

"I—" I start but stop, unsure how to respond. My heart wants to say yes, but my mind is telling me to be cautious. Mal made a vow to me before, and he broke it. And even though he had his reasons, I cannot bring myself to let go of the pain and anger of his betrayal just yet. So instead of offering him a simple yes or no, I give him the most honest answer I can. "I need time to consider."

His gaze holds mine a moment before he dips his head in a subtle nod. *"Rest,"* he whispers. *"I will keep watch. And tomorrow, we will find you some clothing and we will send a raven to your grandmother, telling her you are well."*

Closing my eyes, I nestle into Mal's side. Memories flit to the surface of my mind of days past when we used to explore the woods together, taking afternoon naps in a meadow or on the banks of a river. Those were days of contentment and peace. Of dappled sunlight filtering through the trees, and the naïve happiness of youth… of believing life would always be full of such beautiful days. After a while, I allow myself to drift away into sleep.

* * *

As my mind slowly comes back into awareness, the smell of a campfire and roasted meat fills my senses. I open my eyes and see Mal, in his two-legged form, tending the fire spit, turning what looks like was once a hare over the open flames.

He is dressed in dark pants that I know are conjured with his shape-shifting abilities, and his upper body is completely bare. Warmth flushes through me as my gaze travels over the thick cords of muscle that cover his broad shoulders, torso, and arms. He is masculine perfection made manifest before me.

He twists to reach for something, and I notice a strange black symbol on his back.

As if sensing I'm awake, his pointed left ear turns in my direction a moment before he glances over his shoulder. "I caught us breakfast," he says proudly. "I figured you might be hungry."

I push myself up to sitting, and he hands me a strip of cooked meat. The familiar scent of *brynlar* touches my nostrils and a faint smile curls my lips.

"I flavored it with that herb you like," he says proudly. "I found a whole field of it growing in a clearing nearby."

I take a tentative bite, and an appreciative hum leaves my mouth as the delicious flavor rolls across my tongue. Memories flood my mind of all the time we used to spend together.

He was always thoughtful like this, flavoring my food just the way he knew I liked it. It's been so long since I had this. "This is so good," I murmur between bites.

Mal flashes a devastatingly handsome smile that makes my heart flutter.

How is it that he still has this effect on me after all this time?

He turns and uses his claws to slice off a few more strips of meat, and when he does, I notice the mark on his back again. "What is that symbol on your back?"

"A protective rune," he replies. "Most of us got them during the war when Avalor started using Mages to fight their battles."

"You said most," I point out. "Why wouldn't everyone get this rune for protection?"

"It is… very painful."

It must be horrible indeed. Mal has never been one to complain.

"But worth it," he continues. He tips up his chin. "As my mate, the protection extends to you and any pups we may have later on."

At the mention of children, I lower my gaze, unable to meet his eyes as my cheeks flush with heat. My mind replays the memory of his kiss and the feeling of his body against mine, the last day we were together before I had to escape with my family.

Many times, I have imagined a future where he took me then, claiming me completely that night in the woods.

Most couples conceive during the mating chase, and I often wonder if the same would have been true for us.

"There is a river nearby where we can drink if you are thirsty," he says, interrupting my thoughts.

While I am quite parched, I have another need I must attend to first. The slight twinge in my bladder is becoming more insistent now that I'm awake. "I'll be right back," I tell him as I stand.

"I'll come with you."

"No." I frown. "I will be fine."

He opens his mouth to protest, but I interrupt. "This is not the first time I've ever had to relieve myself in the woods, Malak."

"Yes, but we were not being hunted then, as we may be now," he counters. "If your betrothal is as important to him and his father as I think it is, the prince could have dozens of his warriors trailing us. And we are not familiar with these woods. Any number of dangers could be lurking here," he presses. "I will stand far enough away to give you privacy, but close enough to be on watch in case—"

"I do not need you to stand guard," I reply. "I promise not to go far."

Crossing his arms over his chest, he narrows his eyes, considering. "Fine. But call out immediately if you need anything."

I stop short of rolling my eyes. "I will."

In the past this level of caring used to make me feel special. Now, it is only a painful reminder of what we used to have between us... before he broke my heart. Part of me knows that he is only trying to protect me, but another chafes at the thought, because now I understand that his idea of protection includes shattering my heart for the sake of keeping me safe. If I'd had a choice, I would rather have known he still loved me, rather than believing he'd broken his promise to love me always.

I make sure to keep the campfire in sight as I make my way through the woods. The gentle roar of running water echoes through the forest, growing louder the further I walk. Moving behind a large trunk, I dart a glance around me to make sure no one and nothing is nearby before I finally relieve myself.

When I'm finished, I walk back around the tree and nearly collide with Malak. "What are you doing here?" I ask, unable to hide the irritation in my tone.

"You said you would not go far," he replies accusingly.

"I could still see our camp." I gesture angrily toward the fire.

He growls low in his throat. "You are mine to protect. And I will not—"

"I'm *not* yours." I cut him off, and his eyes widen slightly. "You lost the right to call me that when you sent your letter." The angry words leave my mouth without thinking.

I hate that we are having this argument again, but I cannot let go of the pain and the hurt. I've carried it for too long. It's burned into my very heart, and I wonder now if it will ever truly heal.

"You carry my mark," he states firmly. "That means that you are—"

"You told me to move on without you. Or did you forget?"

"I had no choice, Luna. My father—"

"Yes, you did," I snap. "You could have used our code to tell me the truth."

Traitorous tears threaten to fall, but I keep them in. I do not want to be this bitter person, but every time he insists that he sent me that devastating letter to protect me, I lash out without thinking.

"I gave you my heart and you let me believe that I was *nothing* to you. And now you're here... and you expect me to just fall back into your arms as if you never hurt me. As if you never shattered my heart. So, you do not get to call me yours," I repeat bitterly. "And I can take care of myself, Mal. While you were *protecting* me from your father, I was left with this." I tilt my head to the side, baring my neck and his mark. "You asked why I covered it. It's because it made me a target—an outcast among my own people. So, I had to hide it." I level an angry glare at him. "And I do not need *you* to *protect* me. You left me. For three years, you were gone. So, no, I do not need you, Mal," I practically spit out the words. "I am perfectly capable of protecting myself."

Without waiting for him to respond, I turn and head toward the river. Dappled sunlight spears through the trees, reflecting off the turbulent water as it flows through the heart of the woods. When I reach the river's edge, I dip both hands into the crystalline liquid and wash my face before drinking.

I stare down at my reflection and heave a sigh. Why can't I just let go of my anger? Why can I not just be happy that he's here? In truth, I missed him. Terribly. But as I study myself, I realize the truth. It's because I'm waiting for it again. Bracing myself for him to leave me like he did before. It was so painful when he left, and I'm afraid of risking my heart only to have it shattered once more.

A strange ripple cuts through the flowing water against the current, pulling me back from my thoughts. Cold fear sweeps down my spine as a distorted face with pitch black eyes and shimmering green scales peers up at me from the river's depths. Its lips pull back in a feral grin, revealing two rows of black, razor-sharp fangs.

"Malak!" I cry out, stumbling back from the edge. I twist onto my stomach to push up from the ground, but something wet and slimy wraps around my ankle in an iron grip, jerking me back. I claw at the ground as it drags me toward the water's edge.

"Luna!" Mal races toward me, his eyes wide with panic.

Desperate to escape, I kick out with my free leg at the dark, webbed hand that holds me, but it's no use. A terrified cry rips from my throat as dagger sharp, black claws dig into my ankle, pulling me into the water.

My eyes lock with Mal's and the world shifts into slow motion as cold water envelopes me, cutting off my scream as I'm dragged into the icy depths.

CHAPTER 13

MALAK

My pulse pounds in my ears as I race toward her. Luna's desperate, terror-filled eyes lock with mine, her terrified scream cutting off abruptly as she's dragged beneath the surface.

Lunging forward, I jump into the river. The icy water stings my skin as I dive in. The water is cold and murky as I track the outline of the monstrous creature dragging my mate deeper into the water.

My limbs burn as I fight against the current. The torrent swirls, dragging me downstream. Sharp pain ripples across my side as I slam against rock. Luna's muffled screams tear at my heart as I go tumbling along the riverbed before righting myself again.

Panicked, I scan the water for my beloved. A flash of light catches on the monster. A Kelpie. Its dark scales shimmer briefly before winking out. Pitch-black eyes meet mine as it bares its sharp fangs. Its webbed hands are wrapped solidly around Luna, sharp claws digging into her tender flesh.

My mate is strong and brave, despite her terror. Black blood swirls in the water as she stabs her captor repeatedly with a sharp rock, struggling to break free.

I call upon every bit of my strength and push toward them. Swiping out with my claws, I catch its side. The Kelpie releases an ear-piercing shriek as I slice his chest.

Enraged, the Kelpie releases Luna and rushes toward me. We clash in a blur of fangs and claws, locked in a deadly embrace. The churning river drags us along the riverbed. Sharp rocks stab and scrape at my skin as his claws rip into my flesh, but I refuse to let him go. He dared to hunt my mate and now I will make certain he hunts no more.

Closing my eyes, I shift into my wolf form. Sinking my teeth deep into his neck, I jerk my head and snap his bones. Cold satisfaction floods my veins as the light leaves his eyes and he goes still.

I release his body and search for Luna. I spot her immediately, her arms and legs flailing wildly as the turbulent water sweeps her toward a group of submerged boulders. Alarm bursts through me, and I push off from the riverbed, pumping my legs furiously as I swim, desperate to reach her.

I catch her skirt with my fangs and pull her toward me, spinning at the last second to place myself between her and the rocks. The air explodes from my lungs as my back slams against the boulders with an audible crack beneath the water.

Shifting back into my two-legged form, I force myself to focus despite the pain. Looping one arm around Luna's waist, I push up from the riverbed. We break the surface, and I pump my limbs furiously to reach the shore.

I pull Luna out of the water and onto the riverbank. She coughs and sputters, completely soaked and shivering as she draws in great gulping breaths of air. Blood seeps through her wet clothing from the puncture wounds on her torso, left behind by the Kelpie's claws. "We must get you warm," I tell her. "We—"

She turns and wraps her arms around my neck, her body shaking with hiccupping sobs.

I brush the hair back from her face, as I hold her to my chest. "You are safe now."

"You could have died." She draws in a shaking breath.

"A small price to pay so that you may live," I whisper into her hair, thankful that she is alive and breathing.

"Do not say that," her voice quavers as she holds me even tighter.

"I could have lost you," I barely manage as terror grips my heart anew. "Do you not know that you are everything to me?"

The saline scent of her tears grows stronger, burning my nostrils. Cupping her jaw, I force her gaze to mine. "Have you so little faith in me?" I tease lightly. Tipping up my chin, I puff my chest out exaggeratedly. "I am brave and strong, and"—I arch a teasing brow—"extremely difficult to kill."

A huff of laughter escapes her even as tears stream down her cheeks. I drop my forehead gently to hers, threading my fingers through her damp hair. "We are safe now, Luna," I whisper. "All is well."

Her teeth chatter lightly, and I growl low in my throat. My mate is freezing and injured, and I need to get her warm before she becomes ill. But first, I must get her out of these wet clothes. "You need to undress."

Her eyes widen, and I expect her to protest. I'm shocked when she nods in agreement. Her hands tremble and her fingers shake as she tries to remove her clothing. I grip the hem of her gown and pull it up over her body, leaving her in only the small scraps of cloth that cover her breasts and her pelvis. The material hits the ground with a wet slap.

Many times, I have dreamed of having her bare before me, but not like this. Despite her coldness, her cheeks are flushed bright red in embarrassment.

Her people are not like mine. Nudity—even partial nakedness—is frowned upon in their culture, so I avert my gaze, not wanting to embarrass her any further. I have never understood why humans are so ashamed of their bodies, but my kind learned long ago that it was necessary to conjure the appearance of clothing when having any interactions with them.

I throw her sodden clothing over my shoulder and then pluck her from the ground. She gasps as I hoist her to my chest, but she says nothing. A low rumble of approval vibrates my throat when she tucks her head under my chin and curls into me, instinctively seeking warmth.

Fierce protectiveness fills me. I am both awed and humbled by her trust in me to care for her.

My ribs ache from the impact on the rocks. I grit my teeth at the pinch of pain along my side as I step over a fallen trunk. As much as I want to, I cannot risk shifting into my wolven form until I am healed. If I do, my injuries could become permanent.

Fortunately, my kind heal quickly, and the damage done to my body by the rocks should be healed by tomorrow.

My inner wolf is on edge. The instinct to protect my mate a primal need that burns within as I scan the woods for any signs of danger.

A cool breeze blows through the forest, and my heart stops when I catch the scent of at least a dozen men and tracking hounds.

"What is it?" she asks.

"We are being hunted," I snarl. "It seems the prince does not want to let you go. His men are still far away, but we need to move. If we remain here, they are likely to discover us."

I need to find somewhere to shelter and build a fire. Somewhere secure, where I can leave Luna to get warm while I search for herbs to treat her wounds. I have never looked down upon her because she is human, but this is one of the few times I wish she were a Wolf-Shifter. If she were, her wounds would already be healing, like mine.

As quickly as I can, I pick my way through the forest. I take the opportunity to cross several small streams along our path. This should make it harder for the hounds to track our scent. The dull roar of water draws my attention. As much as I wish to avoid the chance of possibly running into another Kelpie, I also know that Luna cannot go without water as long as I can. It is better for my mate if we remain close to a source of water.

"I can walk, Mal," she says. "You don't have to carry me."

I know she is strong. I saw how she fought the Kelpie. But I nearly lost her, and right now I wish only to hold her close. My inner wolf will be satisfied with nothing else but her nearness until he is calm again.

"You are not a burden," I tell her. "And I know you can walk, but I am faster, Luna. Trust me."

Her eyes search mine a moment before she nods. "All right."

After what feels like forever, we reach a large waterfall. The river spills over the edge of a cliff, crashing into the collecting pool up ahead before continuing on its winding path through the woods. The deafening roar of the water cascading down the rock face drowns out all other noise.

Carefully, I make my way around the edge of the collecting pool until I reach the rock wall and follow it into the forest. A yawning cave mouth up ahead seems promising. It is far enough from the water that a kelpie is unlikely to catch us unaware, but close enough to the river that I can easily retrieve water for my mate.

Kelpies are rather solitary creatures, preferring to hunt alone. Hopefully, the one we encountered earlier is the only one that claimed this river as its territory.

As we approach the cave, the opening is a jagged archway, carved into the rockface. Shadow and mist shroud the entrance. Cautiously, I approach, tipping my head up and scenting the air for any signs of danger.

I detect the smell of ash and burned wood. Peering into the darkness, I watch for any movement, searching for signs that this cave may already be occupied by someone or something else.

When I am satisfied that there is nothing, I cautiously enter, holding Luna close. The sound of the nearby waterfall grows faint as we venture deeper, replaced by the dripping of water echoing throughout the cavern. The air is damp and oddly warm as well, and I notice the remains of a campfire further in.

My nostrils flare at the scent of another, but it is faint. Whoever was here, they have been gone at least two or three days. Fortunately for us, they left a stack of kindling and larger branches to make another fire, along with a firestone to ignite the wood.

"We can shelter here for the night," I tell her. "The prince's guards and their hounds should have lost our scent by now, but we will remain here to be sure. It should be safe to leave in the morning."

Soft light filters in from outside, but not enough to illuminate the entire cave. My eyes quickly adjust to the low lighting as I explore the back of the cavern. The ceiling is so low I have to bend down to walk.

"It's warmer here," Luna remarks. "What do you see?" she asks, reminding me that she cannot see in the dark as I can.

Moisture clings to our skin, and as we walk further in, I discover the source. "Several small pools."

Each one is filled with crystal-clear water. One appears big enough that we could use it to bathe. It is also shallow enough that Luna should be able to touch the bottom.

Light mist swirls across the surface, and as we move closer, I notice the stone floor is growing warmer beneath my feet. "These must be fed by a hot spring," I muse. "You should be comfortable here while I start a fire."

Luna nods, and I carefully set her on the ground. She quickly draws her knees up to her chest, and my heart clenches as she blinks, unseeing into the darkness. I know she's still shaken from what happened earlier, and she has every right to be. She nearly drowned.

She is hurt, and yet, she does not complain. But then again, Luna has always been this way. She is strong, and she is brave.

I also know that she hates the dark, and so I make a point of talking to her while I work on making a fire. "Once I am finished with the fire, I will search for some herbs to treat your wounds," I explain. "I noticed some *cavo* in the woods that I can use to make a poultice. It should help with the healing."

I'm so thankful that I paid attention when we were younger. Luna cut herself on a rock once and I observed as the healer treated her wound with a poultice made from cavo leaves. My kind rarely need the help of a healer unless a wound is severe.

It doesn't take long for the kindling to catch and even less time for it to spread into a roaring fire as I stack more branches on the hearth. I turn back to Luna. Her legs are still drawn up to her chest and her chin is resting on her knees.

I drape her wet clothing on a large rock nearby for it to dry and then kneel down beside her. She lifts her gaze to mine, and she appears so vulnerable in this moment it nearly breaks me. "Are you sure we're safe here?"

I nod. "I scent no one nearby." I turn my gaze to the cave mouth. "I must gather some herbs to treat your wounds."

"I'm fine," she says.

The raw angry marks on her skin suggest otherwise. "I will not go far," I promise.

"Mal." She grips my forearm. "Please, don't go."

My heart clenches. "I have to."

"No, you don't," she counters. "I'm fine."

I glance pointedly at the claw marks on her arms and the ones on her side. "No, you are not."

Clenching her jaw, she lowers her gaze to the floor. "I've had worse," she murmurs. "Trust me. I will be fine. I don't want you to get hurt or caught."

I love that she is worried for my safety because it means that, despite her anger, she still cares for me. Hope flares in my chest at the thought that perhaps she still loves me as I love her.

Even if she does not, it is enough for me that she allows me to care for her. That kind of trust is one of the greatest honors a female Wolf-Shifter can give to a male in my culture.

"I'll be fine." My brow furrows deeply. "What do you mean you've had worse?"

She shakes her head softly. "Never mind," she murmurs.

I wait a moment for her to speak. When she does not, I decide not to press her. I head for the exit. The sooner I leave, the faster I can return to her. "I will stay close to the cave," I reassure her.

She nods, but does not look up at me.

* * *

MAKING sure to stay within sight of the cavern, it doesn't take long to find what I need to treat her. Quickly, I make my way back to the cave. When I enter, she startles slightly before relaxing again.

Grinding the leaves between two rocks, they form a medicinal paste. I rip a strip of fabric from her still drying gown and dip it into the water to cleanse it. Carefully and methodically, I begin treating her wounds, starting with the ones on her arms before moving to her torso.

She remains still as I work, and I keep my touch light and efficient, trying to make her comfortable. I know she is embarrassed to be only partially dressed, and I want her to know that this is not about anything but tending to her.

Luna is my mate and I want only to care for her and protect her. Each puncture wound fills me with fear. I nearly lost her. My inner wolf is restless. The desire to get Luna to the Vale—to safety is overwhelming. If I thought she could stand the journey, I would continue on through the night, carrying her the entire way. But she is hurt, and she needs to rest for at least a few hours before we continue.

When I'm finally finished, I check on her clothing. Her sleep gown is dry, but her robe is still damp. I move back to her side and hand the gown to her, and she quickly slips it back on. She rubs her hands up and down her arms, still cold despite the fire.

I lament again that I cannot shift into my four-legged form, to warm her. The pain along my ribs is tolerable, but I must wait at least a few more hours before I shift. I cannot risk damaging myself further, by transforming before I am healed. And I need to be able to change forms when we travel tomorrow, so I may carry her on my back.

Luna squeaks in surprise as I pull her into my lap so that her legs are across my thighs, and wrap my arms tightly around her. "I will keep you warm."

Instead of arguing, like I expect, she nestles into me. "Thank you." She sighs and relaxes in my arms, and I love how comfortable she is with me like this. That she knows I would never hurt or take advantage of her.

"Do you remember the fort we tried to build when we were younger?" she asks.

I chuckle softly. "You mean the one that collapsed when Fredrik knocked it down because we would not let him in?"

"Yes, that one." She laughs and then glances around the cavern. "This cave would have been perfect for us."

"And more easily defended from my brother." I laugh again.

"What happened to him?" she asks. "I heard rumors that he tried to conquer the kingdom of Eryadon."

"It is a long story," I tell her. "He was deceived by a Blood Witch, disguised as a human. She ensorcelled him and he thought she was his mate, but it was all a lie. She used him to try to take the kingdom from Princess Lyana." I pause. "By the time he discovered the truth, and was freed from her spell, he'd been injured. He ordered our warriors to retreat, and came back to Winterhold in shame and full of pain and sadness."

"Is he all right?" she asks. "Is Eryadon an enemy now of Winterhold?"

"Once they realized that he'd been under the Blood Witch's dark spell, he made peace with Queen Lyana and her mate, King Caelen. His physical health is improved, but his heart, I believe, will take some time to recover. The Blood Witch made him believe they were mated."

I lean back against the cavern wall. "He admitted to me, shortly after, that he was always so jealous of us. You and I were always together, and he said he wished he had what we did. And while under the Blood Witch's spell, he believed that is what he had found. But it was all a devastating lie."

She swallows hard. "I'm sorry for him. A broken heart is a hard thing to mend."

I wince inwardly, for I know she is not just speaking of my brother.

"There was a moment during the war," she begins, her gaze fixed on the ground with a faraway look. "Winterhold had taken the capital, and Mother and I were hiding in a cellar with several others. And for a moment, I felt like you were there. Almost as if my heart were insisting that you were nearby." She shakes her head softly. "The feeling was so strong I was tempted to go up the stairs… to call out for you."

I still, studying her in disbelief. Two bonded Wolf-Shifters can sense each other when they are near, but I did not know this was possible between a human and one of my kin. But there can be no other explanation for what she felt. It had to be our bond. "I was there when we took the capital, Luna."

Her eyes snap to mine, and I continue. "I felt it too." I place my hand to my chest, directly over my heart. "I thought it was longing or hope that I would find you. But now, I believe it was our bond."

"You were the reason they let our people go, when Winterhold invaded the capital, weren't you?" she asks softly.

I nod. "When our warriors flanked the capital, we wondered why Avalor's army did not retreat. They were severely outnumbered and losing badly. But we quickly realized that the reason they refused to give up was because they were protecting their families that were trapped in the city."

"Our king was a fool." Her expression hardens. "He insisted Winterhold would never take the capital. And when it happened, he fled with the prince and their guards. They left us there to die."

"He was a coward," I agree. "When we learned your own leaders had abandoned your people, I gave orders to allow the evacuation of civilians to the south and to provide them with food and supplies."

"Those supplies kept us alive through the worst of it. Your orders saved so many families."

She does not realize that my orders also ended many lives. "I am the one who demanded the execution of your king and the prince," I admit, bracing myself for her judgment. When she says nothing, I continue. "When I learned they had abandoned your people to save themselves, I instructed our warriors to hunt them down and end them."

I curl my hands into fists at my sides at the memory of the blind loyalty of Avalor's generals. They truly believed their king would return. They could not fathom that their monarch had abandoned them when they needed them most.

"My men caught up to them at the southern port, readying to sail away to save themselves. I knew if we did not kill them, your armies would never surrender. They would valiantly have fought to their deaths for a king and his heir who cared nothing of their sacrifice. It was the only way to end the war quickly."

I meet her gaze evenly. "My father wanted them brought to him for torture and public execution, but that would have only dragged things on much longer, and I wanted it over. I wanted the war to end as fast as possible so I could search for you."

I take her hand. "It was agony wondering where you were, Luna. And I prayed to the goddess every day that she would keep you safe. Keep you warm. Keep you fed." I clench my jaw. "Every decision I made, every order I gave, and every mercy I granted... all of it was because of you. I could not stand the thought of you suffering. Of you cold, and scared, and alone, and hurt."

Through our connection, I sense her sadness, so strong it is as if a hole has been carved in my chest. "What is wrong?"

"I understand now just how much you were trying to protect me, Mal." Cautious hope blooms deep within as her eyes search mine. "But I need you to understand something too."

"What is it?"

"So many people hated me because of this." She gestures to my mark on her neck. "Especially during the war. But I didn't care because I knew what it meant. It was sacred. A promise that you loved me. A vow that you would come for me someday.

"And so I endured all the hatred and anger that was directed at me by my own kind. Because what *we had* was stronger than all of it. Through the war and the death of my parents, your mark was the promise I held onto when everything was crumbling all around me.

"It was my hope when we were hiding in cellars while your kingdom invaded and sacked the city. It was my comfort when I felt lost. It was my light in the darkness when I was afraid."

Tears stream down her cheeks. "And your letter took all of that away in an instant." She draws in a shaking breath. "When I first received it, I thought it was a blessing that it found me in the middle of everything that was going on. But after I read it, I wished it had never come to me. It would have been better to have been left wondering, than to have known there was no hope of the future that I had been holding on for."

Sharp pain lances my heart at the depths of her pain and sadness. Tears gather at the corners of my eyes as shame and guilt wash through me. She is my mate and in trying to protect her, I caused her so much pain and anguish. I hurt she who is most precious to me. "Forgive me," I whisper. "I meant only to protect you, Luna. I—"

"What about my heart, Mal? We swore ourselves to each

other. I trusted you with my heart and you cast it aside as if it were nothing. And now you ask me to entrust it to you again."

Tears sting my eyes as her pain and despair are laid bare before me. And all of it, by my own hand. *Me.* The one who was supposed to cherish and protect her from harm. Always.

Cupping the back of her head, I drop my forehead to hers, clenching my jaw as her words settle in my chest like a heavy stone. She is my mate, and I hurt her. Deeply.

"I broke your trust, Luna." Sadness tears my chest. "And I will never forgive myself for it. But I vow that if you will give me a chance, I will show you that I am worthy of your heart again. Please, my beautiful mate. Please, give me the chance to prove myself to you."

"I worked so hard to move on, after your letter." Her voice quavers. "And I thought that I finally had. But then you arrived at the ball… You turned my entire life upside down."

She shakes her head softly, fighting back tears. "You nearly died saving me today, and all I could think was that I was going to lose you all over again." She touches my cheek. "And I don't want to lose you, Mal."

Her gaze holds mine as she leans in and brushes her lips to my own. They are soft and warm, just as I remembered. She threads her fingers through my hair as her mouth parts against mine and I curl my tongue around hers, deepening our kiss.

"I've been holding onto my hurt and my pain and my anger for so long, Mal. But when I almost lost you, I realized that I needed to let it go. I love you," she whispers between kisses. "I love you so much, Mal."

"Even after everything?" I ask, surprised that she would still trust me with her heart after all the pain I caused her.

"Goddess help me," she whispers against my lips. "I never stopped."

My inner wolf rises within, desperate to claim her, as happiness brighter than a thousand stars burns in my chest. She moans lightly as I explore her mouth. Gripping her waist, I lift her body and turn her to face me, her thighs now straddling my hips.

My *stav* is hard and painfully erect, and she gasps at the press of my solid length against her soft folds. The thin triangle of silk that separates me from her entrance is warm and damp with her arousal. My nostrils flare as I drink in her delicious scent.

She is mine. My inner wolf howls, demanding that I claim my mate. The primal need to sink deep into her warm, wet heat and fill her with my essence is so intense it is nearly overwhelming.

I tighten my left arm around her waist and grip the long, silken strands of her hair between my fingers with the other, as she molds her perfect form to mine. A deep growl rumbles in my chest as she rolls her hips against my own.

Fierce possessiveness fills me. It takes every bit of my control not to flip her onto her stomach. The instinct to bury my length deep inside her channel, cover her with my body, and knot her until she carries my pups burns like fire in my veins.

She is perfect and everything inside me wants to claim her completely: body, mind, heart, and soul. Her heart pounds, and her breathing quickens as she moves against me, and my hips rise to meet hers.

Our kisses become more urgent as we move as one. Sweat beads across my brow as I struggle to hold back my release. I refuse to climax before she has found her pleasure.

I reach between us and slip my fingers beneath the silken material between her thighs. She inhales sharply when I brush my thumb over the sensitive pearl of flesh at the apex.

"More," she pants, digging her nails into my shoulders. "Please, Mal."

My knot expands. The instinct to fill her with my essence so strong that I worry I'll come before her. I growl as I concentrate my touch on the areas that make her entire body light up with pleasure.

CHAPTER 14

LUNA

Desire coils tight in my core, and I cling to Mal as pleasure builds deep within. It's so intense, it makes me afraid. My every nerve ending is on fire, and I hover on the edge of a precipice, both anxious and fearful of giving myself over to it entirely. "Mal," I barely manage. "Mal, please," I whisper, but I'm not even sure what I'm asking him for.

"Show me how to touch you," he breathes against my lips.

I reach between us, guiding him to the spot that is most sensitive. A startled cry escapes my lips as everything becomes more intense.

I wrap my hand around his length, and he's so large my fingers don't quite meet. A small stream of liquid pulses from the tip, coating my hand. "Luna," he grinds out. "My stav is sensitive. If you do not stop, I'll be unable to hold back my release."

"I want you to feel what I do," I whisper. "I want you near the edge with me, Mal."

He hisses through his fangs as I trace my fingers over the knot at the base, feeling it expand beneath my touch. The thought of our bodies joined and locked together sends me over the edge, and I cry out his name as waves of pleasure wash over and through me.

His stav expands and then begins to pulse in my hand. He roars out my name and thick ropes of seed erupt from the tip, coating my abdomen and pelvis. The fluid is sticky and warm against my skin and feels as if it goes on forever before it finally stops.

Panting heavily, he drops his forehead to my own. He smooths his hand over my body, covering me with his essence. His stav is hard and his knot is still expanded when it begins to pulse again, erupting once more. His eyes are full of fiery possession as he leans in and captures my mouth in a claiming kiss.

Gently, he lays us both down. When he turns onto his side to face me, he sucks in a sharp breath.

"You're hurt," I whisper, remembering how he saved me from the river rocks, hurting himself in the process. "We should not have—"

He silences me with a kiss, and then rolls me onto my stomach. He covers my body with his. Desire ripples down my spine at the warm press of his solid, muscular form against mine. He kisses my neck and whispers in my ear. "I will never be too injured to worship my mate."

A rumbling growl of approval rises in his throat as I tilt my head to the side, offering him better access as he traces his tongue lightly across my skin, his fangs grazing the mark he made three years ago. Warm fluid spreads across my lower back and I twist my head to look up at him, surprised. "How many times do you—"

"The need to fully claim you is strong." He dips his nose

to the curve of my neck, inhaling deeply. "It is instinct, and my body is responding to this."

I go still, wondering at his statement. He said the need to claim me is strong and yet... he did not fully claim me, and I don't understand why.

Worry seeps into my chest as the painful memory of his rejection letter resurfaces in my thoughts.

He nuzzles my temple and then gently rolls me onto my back. Mal lies down beside me and tugs me to his chest. He smooths a hand down my arm. "What is wrong?"

Prince Duren is hunting us. He believes he needs me to secure the throne, and I doubt he'll give up easily. Mal left me before, when he believed it was the best way to protect me. The fact that he did not claim me fully... I cannot help but think he is holding back. That, perhaps, he has changed his mind, and decided to take me somewhere to safety, only to leave me again.

I want so much to ask, but I cannot bring myself to do it, for fear of his answer.

Sighing heavily, I force these dark thoughts away and snuggle into his warmth. If this is all the time that I will have with him, I'll cherish every moment. "Nothing," I lie. "I'm simply tired."

It's not a complete falsehood. I *am* exhausted, but I do not want to sleep. Part of me is worried that this is some sort of dream. That I'll wake up and he'll be gone.

That day may still come, I think darkly before forcing my worry back down again.

CHAPTER 15

MALAK

T he need to provide for my mate is a call I cannot ignore. When I wake, Luna is still asleep. I skim my nose along her neck and breathe deep. She is my mate, and my inner wolf is pleased beyond measure that she carries our scent. He is calmer now than he has been in the past three years we've been apart, but he will not be truly settled until I have claimed her fully.

I carefully untangle myself from her and then go out in search of game. It doesn't take long to find another hare and bring it back to the cave.

I'm already roasting it on the fire spit when she finally awakens. She gives me a sleepy smile. "That smells delicious."

I quickly carve the choicest bits with my claws and feed them to her. When we're finished, she walks to the pool in the back of the cave, insisting she needs a bath.

My inner wolf snarls at the thought of her washing my scent from her skin. But she is human. Scent marking is not important to them like it is among wolves.

My mouth goes dry as I watch her lower herself into the water, my gaze traveling over the soft curves of her body. We really should be leaving as soon as possible, but the temptation to join her is one I cannot resist. She is mine, and now that I am allowed to touch her, I can think of nothing else I'd rather do. Ever. For the remainder of my existence.

I walk to the water, and her cheeks flush a deep red hue as she looks up at me. "May I join you?"

Softly biting her lower lip, she nods, and I slip into the pool. Luna is still shy, it seems, despite what we shared last night. I reach my hand out, and she takes it. Gently, I pull her to me. Placing two fingers under her chin, I study her lovely face before I seal my mouth over hers.

Our kiss is soft and tender at first, but when she wraps her legs around my waist, my control snaps. My inner wolf is ravenous, desperate to touch her, to taste her, to claim her.

I rip my mouth from hers and kiss a heated trail down her neck to the valley between her breasts. I cup one soft globe in my palm as I close my mouth over the tip of the other. She moans as I flick my tongue over the hardened peak. "Mal," she breathes. "That feels so good."

She kneads the muscles of my shoulders as I move my attention to the other breast. I have dreamed of this for so long, and I will not waste any opportunity to worship her body.

As much as I want to fully claim her, her scent tells me that she is nearing the fertile peak of her cycle. We have not spoken of pups yet, and I do not want to assume anything without speaking to her first. But even if we cannot fully mate right now, I want only to give her pleasure. I want her to crave my touch. I want her as addicted to me as I already am to her.

Her scent calls to my inner wolf. Desperate to taste her, I lift her out of the water and set her on the edge of the pool.

She looks down at me in confusion as I guide one leg over my shoulder. "Open for me," I growl softly. "I want to taste you."

My ears detect the quickening beat of her heart as she gives me a small nod. I slide my hands up her inner thighs, parting them and baring her to my gaze. My nostrils flare as I drink in her delicate scent. She is perfect, and she is mine, and I want nothing more than to worship my mate and taste her sweet nectar upon my tongue.

CHAPTER 16

LUNA

Mal's eyes remain locked on mine as he guides my other leg over his shoulder and then lowers his head between my thighs. I gasp and dig my heels into his back as he drags his tongue through my folds. A spark of intense pleasure ripples through me when he reaches the small bundle of nerves at the apex.

A low growl of approval vibrates in his throat as he begins to feast on me. It is too much and not enough all at once as he teases his tongue over my sensitive flesh. I reach for him, and he threads his fingers through mine as I writhe beneath his attentions.

Nothing exists outside of this moment as he balances me on the razor-sharp edge of desire, holding me there while everything deep inside tightens in anticipation.

His eyes lift to mine, and he swirls his tongue over the small pearl of flesh that drives my pleasure even higher. I fall into blissful oblivion as my release washes through me like a giant wave.

My head falls back, and I'm panting heavily, reveling in the small aftershocks of my release when he lifts out of the water and pulls me into his lap, my thighs resting on either side of his hips. His stav is a hard bar between us. I'm completely and thoroughly sated, but I want him. I want everything.

I wrap my arms around his neck, kissing him long and deep. "I want you," I murmur between kisses. "So much."

A sharp hiss escapes through his fangs as I roll my hips into his.

He grips my thighs firmly, holding me still. His heated gaze meets mine before he drops his forehead gently to my own. "We should go," he rasps. "We have much ground to cover today."

It's difficult, but I bite back my disappointment. I wonder again why he does not fully claim me, and it leaves me unsettled.

I nod and get dressed. Part of me wishes we could stay here longer. We've only been traveling a few days, but I am exhausted. And it feels safe here in our little cave. But I know it is only a temporary safety. We are being hunted and the sooner we reach the Vale, the better.

Mal shifts into his four-legged form, and I study him a moment as he lowers himself to the ground. He used to carry me often, but for some reason, he seems much larger that he was only three years ago. Even lying down on his belly, the top of his back comes up to my chest.

"What is it?" he asks through the bond, cocking his head to one side.

"You seem... bigger than you were before the war."

He puffs out his chest. *"I have grown stronger and more handsome too."*

A smile quirks my lips at his boasting. I grip his fur,

marveling again at how thick and soft it is as I climb atop him. He carefully rises up and turns to me. *"Are you secure?"*

I tighten my legs on his back and lean forward a bit, holding on to the large tufts of fur at the back of his neck and shoulders. The warmth of his body suffuses mine as his masculine scent surrounds me. "Yes."

His powerful muscles bunch and tense beneath my thighs. *"Then hold on."*

He breaks into a run, racing out of the cave and into the forest. The wind whips through my hair and pulls at my form, threatening to rip me off Malak's back. The cold morning air burns my lungs with each inhalation, and my heart pounds with the thrill of excitement as we rush through the woods.

Sunlight filters in through the canopy overhead, casting the forest in an enchanting glow. When we were young, Mal taught me to love the forest and to appreciate nature. Being with him like this is strange in a way. As we race through the woods, memories flood my mind, and it is as if no time has passed… as if the past three years never happened and we'd never been forced apart. He pounds the earth with his massive paws as he races through the forest.

He heads toward a ravine up ahead. *"Hold tightly to me, Luna."*

My heart slams in my throat as he leaps off the edge and lands effortlessly on the cliff across the way, not halting in his speed. Excitement thrums in my veins. It's been so long since I felt this alive, and I release a cry of pure joy and Mal matches it with a sharp howl of his own.

* * *

THE SUN BEGINS its slow descent on the horizon, lengthening the shadows of the trees. Dark clouds form overhead, and rain begins to fall, turning the earth beneath us to muck, forcing Mal to slow his pace.

I pull the hood of my cloak over my head, trying to shield myself from the icy droplets.

The wind picks up and Mal stops. He lifts his head to the sky, his nose twitching as he scents the area. *"The storm is getting worse. We need to find shelter."*

The rain pours down in an unrelenting deluge, drenching us to the bone as we continue through the woods. I shiver as the cold wind whips around us. Closing my eyes, I try to imagine myself in a nice warm bed, with a roaring fire nearby.

Mal stops abruptly, and I open my eyes. "What is—" I start to ask, but the words die in my throat when I notice a small cottage up ahead, nestled amongst the trees. One of the windows is boarded up, and the door is slightly ajar, creaking ominously in the wind.

"It looks abandoned," I tell him. "But... something doesn't seem right."

"I agree," he replies. *"But we do not have a choice. You cannot stay out in this weather."*

"I'll be fine."

He turns back to me. *"We cannot risk you falling ill."* I start to protest, but stop when he adds. *"I have not forgotten how sick you were that time we stayed out in the rain when we were younger. You nearly died then, Luna."*

He's right. So despite my reservations, we make our way towards the cottage, drawn by the promise of shelter from the storm. When we reach the entrance, Mal stops just outside the door. *"Wait here,"* he says. *"I will go inside first."*

Quietly, I slide off his back to wait as he goes inside. As I stand there, my heart pounds in my chest. The forest is dark and foreboding, and eerily silent and still. This place feels unnatural. As if something dark makes its home here.

A low growl stops my heart. *"Run!"* Mal's voice cries out in my head. *"Now!"*

Fear grips me in an iron vise, but I refuse to leave him. Glancing inside, my jaw drops as my mind tries to make sense of what it is seeing. In the dim light, I can barely make out a large red fox as big as Mal.

Its mouth is curled back in a vicious snarl, its fur bristling with anger. They circle each other, fangs bared and claws extended, each waiting for the other to make the first move.

My heart is in my throat as I watch them, my mate in danger and me powerless to help.

Lightning fast, the fox strikes, lunging at Malak with a snarl. Malak dodges and counterattacks, snapping at the fox's flank. They clash together in a tangled mess of fur, claws, and fangs.

Panicked, I search the ground for any sort of weapon, but the only thing nearby is an old wooden broom. I bring it down over my knee, snapping the straw brush from the base to form a makeshift spear. It's not much, but it is better than nothing, and I refuse to leave Mal here to fight alone.

I glance in through a hole in the boarded window. The fox's back is to the door. This is my chance. Steeling myself, I draw in a deep breath and rush through the entry. The fox spins at the last moment with a terrifying growl.

His eyes widen as they meet mine, and he rolls away from my attack, shifting instantly into his two-legged form and slamming against the wall.

Mal transforms immediately and pulls me behind him, growling low in his throat.

"Wait!" The Fox-Shifter raises his hands up in surrender. "I mean you no harm." His reflective orange eyes dart to me, nostrils flaring slightly. "Of course, you are territorial. You are defending your mate," he tells Mal. "I did not understand your aggression, but I understand it now."

Slowly, he stands. Like Mal, he conjures the appearance of clothing. He's dressed in brown trousers with a matching coat that does little to hide the lean but powerful form beneath. He has a long, fluffy red tail with a white tip. Two tufted red fox ears stick up from his matching short red hair. He has a sharp square jaw with an aristocratic nose and brow. He studies Mal warily as he carefully lowers his hands. He cocks his head to one side. "You are Prince Malak of Winterhold, are you not?"

Mal pins him with a dark glare. "Yes," he grits through his teeth. "Who are you?"

The Fox Shifter flashes a friendly smile and makes a slight bow, waving his hand with an exaggerated flourish. "I am Prince Renard of Cambryn, but you may call me Ren."

Mal raises his chin, sniffing at the air. "You were in the cave a few nights ago. I recognize your scent. What are you doing here?"

"The same as you, I suspect." He gestures to the door and the storm outside. "Taking shelter. This place looked abandoned, and"—he looks around the space—"a bit creepy, but I did not have much of a choice if I wanted to get out of the rain."

The interior of the cottage is dark and musty. Cobwebs line the ceilings and windows and the wooden floor could use a good sweep, but at least it's dry and somewhat warm in here. A small bed sits in the far corner with a dust-covered blanket and two wooden rocking chairs are set before the fireplace. Across the room is a small kitchen with a hand water pump that I hope is functioning and a couple rows of shelves on either side of the counter along the wall. They are stacked with a few chipped wooden bowls and cups.

I wonder why these things were left behind. It's obvious whoever lived here did not have much, so it's strange that the few possessions they did have, they chose to leave.

Mal takes a threatening step toward Ren, interrupting my thoughts. His lips curl back in a snarl. "What I mean is: why are you *here*: in this forest?"

"Calm yourself," Ren says. "I am no threat to you or your mate, Prince Malak." He straightens. "I am here because I am on a quest."

"What sort of quest?" Mal presses.

Instead of answering, he gestures to the fireplace. "Perhaps we should start a fire and then we can exchange stories." His eyes sweep to me. "Your mate is human, and you know they do not do well in the cold like this." He dips his chin in slight greeting. "Forgive me. I did not ask your name."

Mal growls. "Do *not* talk to her."

"It's all right, Mal." I rest a hand on his back and then move to his side. "My name is Luna."

He extends his hand, but Mal steps between us, and he lowers it again to his side. Sighing heavily, he rolls his eyes. "She is your mate," he says firmly. "I assure you, I am not trying to coax her away from you."

Mal says nothing, and Ren kneels before the hearth. Fortunately for us, there are stacks of corded wood on the side and a fire starter rock on the mantel. As soon as he gets the fire going, Mal ushers me toward it. "We need to dry your clothes."

I glance at Ren. Even though he's a shifter, and shifters think nothing of nudity, I am not eager to be bare before a stranger. Sensing my concern, Malak pulls the comforter off the bed, shaking it to remove the dust before handing it to me. "You can use this while your clothes dry."

I nod, and he places himself between me and Ren. "Turn around," he commands. "If you dare gaze at my mate while she is changing, I will claw out your eyes."

Ren blinks several times. "I've already told you." He huffs.

"There is no need for threats of violence. I am not going to—"

"Turn. Around. Now," Mal grinds out.

"Fine." Ren huffs again. He turns his back to us, his fluffy tail flicking agitatedly as he waits. "I thought only humans cared about nudity. Not—"

"My mate cares," Mal grits through his teeth. "And so I do too."

"Ah," Ren says. "I understand." He rests his chin on his hand. "You know, I've never understood why humans feel the need to hide their bodies." He shrugs. "Perhaps they think others will find them strange. But in truth, it's not as if they are that different from us," he muses as Mal hangs my clothes on the mantel to dry.

"My people normally only choose to bare ourselves to our mates," I explain. "It is a sign of intimacy."

Mal's expression softens as his eyes meet mine. He wraps the blanket tight around me, and then pulls me into his arms. He settles down in one of the chairs, nestling me into his lap before the fire.

I snuggle into his chest, enjoying the feeling of being held in his arms.

"You can turn around now," I tell Ren.

He sits in the other chair and flashes a warm smile at us. Mal gives him a dark glare in return, and I lightly smack at his shoulder. "Stop," I hiss. "Be nice."

"I *am* being nice," Mal grumbles.

"Well, if this is your version of nice, I cannot imagine what mean would look like," I admonish.

A smile tugs at my lips, and I press a quick kiss to his mouth, trying to reassure him that all is well. My wolf is fierce in his protection of me.

Ren tries but fails to hide a grin. He clears his throat. "If you do not mind my asking, how did you two meet?"

Despite Mal's rumbling chest, I launch into the story of how we met when we were children. When I'm finished, Ren nods. "Friends to lovers," he muses. "My grandparents were the same." Sadness flashes in his eyes, but he quickly averts his gaze.

"Why are you here?" Malak asks again. "You never answered my question."

"As I mentioned," he begins. "I am on a quest." He turns his gaze to the dancing flames. "A seer came to our court. She told me that I must come here. That I must search for an enchanted tower in this particular forest. And in it, would be not only my destiny, but a great treasure that would save our kingdom."

Mal arches a brow. "How do you know she spoke truth?"

"Because I have dreamed of a tower many times before." He shrugs. "I decided it could not simply be coincidence."

My curiosity is piqued. "How long have you been searching?"

"I arrived here a little over a week ago," he explains.

"What if you don't find it?"

"I will not give up until I do," he replies. "Our kingdom is constantly under threat of invasion from the Troll hoards in the North. If there is something that will aid in our defense, I must discover what it is."

"Trolls," Mal grumbles. "They are a plague on these lands."

"I agree," Ren says. "I heard a tale that you drove them off your territory. That you regained the Vale for your people, is that true?"

Mal nods.

Ren's eyes spark with interest. "Impressive. How did you do it?"

"We surprised them," Mal says. "They thought our forces were engaged elsewhere. They were unprepared to meet us in battle."

As Mal and Ren continue to talk, my eyelids blink open and closed as I struggle to stay awake. Leaning back against Mal, I close my eyes.

In his arms, I feel safe and warm. It's been so long since I felt so loved and so cared for. Warmth travels across our bond, wrapping around me like a soothing blanket, and I know it is coming from him. I do my best to project it back, wanting him to know how much I love him.

He rubs his jaw lightly over my temple in an affectionate gesture, and happiness blooms inside me. As he speaks with Ren, his smooth, deep voice rumbles in his chest beneath my ear, lulling me to sleep.

"You are fortunate, Malak," Ren's voice breaks through the fog of my exhaustion. "To have found your mate so early in life."

Mal gently nuzzles the top of my head. "I know," he replies. "She is everything."

Warmth fills my heart and a faint smile curls my lips as I drift away into sleep.

CHAPTER 17

MALAK

Luna falls asleep against my chest and I cannot help but notice Renard's curious eyes on us both. Although his look is one of fascination, it is difficult to bite back a snarl. My inner wolf bristling at the presence of a stranger in our temporary den.

"There are posters of the two of you in Barrywick," Ren says. "You are wanted by the crown."

I narrow my eyes. "If you dare—"

"I am not going to turn you in," he says quickly. "I merely bring it up so that you are aware that there are many who are looking for you. The King has spread word that you abducted Prince Duren's betrothed against her will." He darts a glance at Luna, asleep in my arms. "But I can see clearly that that is not the case. Nevertheless, the reward is... rather significant, so you must take great care to avoid people."

"That is why we are keeping to the forests and the back-roads," I explain.

He leans forward in his seat. "If you are heading to

Winterhold, I must warn you that I came across a house with three Bear-Shifters. They were rather prickly, so if you scent them, it may be best to avoid them entirely." He pauses. "They did mention, however, that there are rumors of a blood witch in these woods." He looks around the cottage. "I half suspect this house may have been hers."

It's bad enough that we have the Prince hunting us, but to know that there may be a Blood Witch claiming this territory is unsettling. I do not bother to correct him that we are traveling to the Vale instead of Winterhold. I trust him not to harm us, but I am reluctant to share our true destination. "Anything else I should be aware of?"

"There were also three Pig-Shifters," he adds. "Brothers. And they were very wary of me, claiming to have had some sort of run in with their Wolf-Shifter neighbor, so they do not trust any predatory shifters."

I roll my eyes. Pig-Shifters can be very dramatic. They always think a predator is out to get them. My father arrested one once on suspicion of theft. He threw him in the dungeon and the pig cried out like a wounded animal all night long, keeping everyone awake in the castle until my father could no longer stand it. He excused his sentence and had him thrown out of the dungeon *and* the kingdom, with a warning never to return.

"Honestly, you'd think I was there to murder them the way they reacted." He sighs. "They were up in arms the moment I set foot on their land. And all I was doing was asking if they knew where the tower was in these woods."

"Did they know?" I ask.

Sighing heavily, he shakes his head. "Almost everyone I've asked has heard rumors of it, but no one has actually seen it."

"Perhaps it is more than a simple enchantment. Maybe it is something as sinister as a spell by a Blood Witch." I give him a pointed look. "Have you considered that possibility?"

"Yes," he replies gravely. "But it is my destiny, so I must press forward."

He is a fool. If I were him, I'd do whatever I could to make certain I never crossed a Blood Witch. They are dangerous creatures, and knowing there may be one nearby makes me even more impatient to reach the Vale. The sooner we're in my lands, the better. Luna will be safe there. I've had the entire castle and surrounding grounds spelled to repel dark magic.

"Is this supposed treasure really worth your life?" I ask.

"If it helps my kingdom repel any further attacks by the Trolls, then yes," he replies without hesitation. He studies me with a piercing gaze. "Surely you understand. You fought them to retake the Vale for your people."

I do not tell him that I am now High Lord of the Vale. He is a prince of Cambryn. When he returns home, he will learn soon enough. They were one of our trading partners, before the Troll invasion, and I have instructed my minister of trade to negotiate with them now that we are rebuilding.

"Have you sent word to your family?" he asks. "Asking for their aid?"

I have not. To do so, I would need access to a courier or a raven.

As if reading my mind, his brow furrows softly. "You've not had a chance, have you?"

"No," I admit.

"I could send a message for you," he offers.

It is tempting, but I am not unsure if I trust him that much. I'm also uncertain that my brother would even send aid. I defied his orders by coming here in the first place. He wanted me to wait. To find a diplomatic way to search for Luna, but I would not be deterred.

My stepping foot on Avalor's soil could force us into another war since I knowingly violated the treaty between our kingdoms. Even more so now that I've stolen Prince Duren's betrothed.

He holds out his hand. "On my honor, I vow that I will not betray you," he says.

Fox-Shifters are known for their sly cunning, but something about this one gives me pause. He appears sincere, and I scent no deception as he speaks, but I cannot be entirely sure.

His eyes dart to Luna, asleep in my arms. "I cared for someone once," he says, sadness softening his features. Closing his eyes briefly, a ripple of light moves across his face, revealing a long, jagged scar across his right cheek. It was hidden before now, with his shifting abilities. "A Troll did this to me, when I fought him to protect her," he explains. "And even though she left me because of it, I would change nothing. Because when someone is important, you will sacrifice anything to protect them."

He looks again at Luna. "If you truly want to protect her, you have to trust someone, Prince Malak. There are too many who hunt you for you to do all of this alone."

He is right. Clenching my jaw, I lean forward. "Know this. If you betray me, and she is hurt because of it, I will hunt you to the ends of the earth, and I will not stop until one of us is dead."

A sharp huff of laughter escapes him. "And I thought Pig-Shifters and Fae were dramatic." He arches a brow and then extends his hand again.

This time, I take it, giving it a firm shake.

CHAPTER 18

LUNA

When I wake in the morning, I'm completely surrounded by warmth. Opening my eyes, I notice a large fluffy black tail draped over me like a blanket and I'm nestled into Malak's side. Yawning, I stretch out and then snuggle into his thick fur.

He gently nuzzles me with his snout. His piercing green eyes search mine. *"Good morning, my beautiful Luna."*

I smile a moment before something catches my eye off to the side. Instinctively, I recoil against Malak before I realize it's Renard coming in the doorway in his fox form.

He shifts instantly and offers me a bright smile. "Good morning." He gestures to the fireplace and the meat roasting on the spit. "I've taken the liberty of catching our breakfast. It should be ready momentarily." His gaze shifts to Mal. "There are no signs of any hunters nearby." He grins. "And I caught a bit of good luck."

"What was it?" I ask.

"I ran across a forest sprite," he says. "She gave me the

name of someone in Barrywick who can help me locate the enchanted tower."

I smile. "I wish you success then."

He dips his chin. "Thank you."

As we sit down to breakfast, he hands me a small pouch. "What is this?"

When I take it from him, the pouch is heavy, and I immediately recognize the weight of the coins inside it.

He looks at me and Malak. "To cross into the Vale, you'll have to go through Bridgemore," he says. "There is an inn called the Sleepy Dragon. It is on this side of the border, and is known for its... discretion given the right amount of coin, of course."

He winks, and Malak growls low in his chest. "I did not say we were traveling to the Vale."

"You didn't have to," Ren quips. "I am well aware that you are the newly appointed High Lord of the Vale, Prince Malak." He arches a brow. "I do not believe there is a soul in Cambryn who did not hear of your victory against the Trolls. And I could have pretended to not know the truth of your destination, but I would not forgive myself if I did not help any way that I could."

"Why does it matter to you?" Mal asks.

"Because I believe in the balance," he replies solemnly.

"What is that?" I ask.

His reflective orange eyes shift to me. "The scales of good and evil," he explains. "All actions have consequences. Every choice we make is weighed in the grand scheme of things."

"I don't understand," I admit.

"Those who choose good—who make the choice to help others—they will one day be repaid in kind." He pauses. "The seer that told me of my destiny and started me on this quest... She granted me this boon because I offered her food when she was disguised as a pauper."

"Why did you do it?"

He frowns. "Why would anyone allow another to starve if they had the means to help them?"

I smile. It is the right answer, and one that tells me he is a good person. I had already suspected as much, but this simply confirms it for me.

Mal would probably believe I am too trusting but there is something about Ren that makes me believe he is telling the truth. "Thank you," I tell him. "Truly."

Mal turns to me. "Ren is going to relay a message to my brother. Would you like him to send one to your grand-mother too?"

I blink several times, shocked that Mal trusts Ren enough to do this, but I am glad. "Yes."

Ren looks at me. "I vow that I will see it done."

I instruct him to send a simple message telling my grand-mother that I am safe, I travel with Mal of my own volition, and that I will send for her once I reach my destination. When I'm done, he dips his chin and then stands. "Well, I should be off." A dashing grin lights his features. "An enchanted tower with my destiny awaits me."

"Good hunting," Mal says.

"Good hunting," Ren replies before bowing with an exag-gerated flourish and shifting back into his fox form. He heads out into the forest, stopping a moment to turn back to us, and I wave. I send a silent prayer to the goddess to guide him on his journey to meet his destiny.

CHAPTER 19

MALAK

I t is less than a day's travel to Bridgemore, but I am already dreading our arrival. According to Ren, there are wanted posters of us everywhere, offering a hefty reward for our capture.

Luna's emotions are a tangle of worry through the bond. She is just as concerned as I am that we may be discovered. When I crossed into Avalor, it was by way of Winterhold. There are several points of entry between those two borders. But between Avalor and the Vale, there are only two, and Bridgemore is the closest.

It is aptly named as the entire city is centered around the bridge that spans the twin mountains. One side of the city is in Avalor, and the other is part of my territory: the Vale.

"Do you think we can cross tonight?" Luna asks.

"It will have to be near midnight, at the changing of the guard on Avalor's side."

* * *

By the time we reach Bridgemore, the sun has already disappeared below the horizon, casting a purple and orange glow over the cobblestone streets and towering buildings. In the center of the city, a magnificent bridge spans the chasm between the two mountains that divide our kingdoms, connecting Avalor to the Vale.

Although it is late, Bridgemore is a hive of activity. The clatter of hooves and the rumbling of carts echo over the expanse as merchants make their way across the bridge, as they pack up their stalls and take their wares home for the day.

I've not had a chance to tour Bridgemore since I became Lord of the Vale, but it is much larger than I remember from when I came here with my father when I was only a pup.

The buildings are a mix of black stone and wood, with steeply slanted roofs and large windows. The gleaming spires of the temple, across the bridge in the Vale, towers above the rest of the city. Once we cross, I will have my warriors find a priest immediately to marry us in the traditions of Luna's people, and have her crowned as Princess of Winterhold and Lady of the Vale—making sure no one questions her status or her titles.

The Vale fortress of Bridgemore lies just beyond the temple—a dark and ominous structure in comparison. Soldiers in the colors of Avalor and the Vale patrol the bridge on their respective sides.

Before we step out of the woods, I shift back into my two-legged form, conjuring the appearance of clothing, complete with a hooded cloak to hide my face. Near the edge of the city, I notice a small home with clothing hanging out on the line in the garden, blowing in the breeze.

"Wait here," I tell Luna.

Before she can ask any questions, I head toward it, moving along the garden wall until I am close enough to grab a thick, fur cloak from the line. I quickly make my way back to Luna and hand it to her.

Anger flashes in her eyes as she snatches it from me. "Are you mad? You could have been caught."

"You need a heavy cloak," I insist. "There are people looking for us, and I will not chance you being caught simply because you do not have the proper attire to conceal your features."

She turns her gaze back to the city and the expansive bridge. "What if we simply try to make a run for it? Try to cross quickly?"

I shake my head. "There are archers positioned on either side. And I am unsure I could message my own people, proving who I am before they'd react to defend our borders."

"What about the inn?" she asks. "Perhaps we should stay there until the changing of the guard."

Although I am reluctant to leave the safety of the forest, the inn is a better choice. It would make it harder for Prince Duren's men to find us if we are already within the city, instead of hovering along the outskirts.

Luna draws the cloak around her shoulders and pulls the hood over her head. I attach the fastening at the front to cover her even more and then tug her to me. "If I tell you to run, you must run. Do you understand?"

"I won't leave you," she protests.

"Luna, please." I pull back just enough to stare deep into her eyes. "I am a Wolf-Shifter. If we are attacked, I would heal faster from an injury than you would. I can buy you time to get away, and I will find you later if we are separated."

"Don't you understand?" she says. "I could not bear the thought of leaving you to face danger alone, Mal. So do not ask this of me." Her small brow furrows softly. "We'll be careful, Mal, and we won't be caught."

I want to believe it's that simple, but the possibility exists that we may be walking into a trap. If Prince Duren suspects we are going to the Vale, he and his men would either already be here or be well on their way to intercept us. My hope is that he believes we are going to Winterhold, to the protection of my brother. "I simply want to be prepared in case we are discovered."

Satisfied with my answer, she nods, but worry still lingers in her eyes. I wish that I could take this from her, but I cannot. All I can do is hope that the moon goddess is on our side.

CHAPTER 20

LUNA

I t doesn't take long to find someone to give us directions to the Sleepy Dragon Inn. We make our way down a narrow, dark alley and come to a stop in front of a ramshackle building. The sign above the door creaks in the wind, and the outer shutters hang half off their hinges.

Malak pushes the door open, and we walk inside.

Raucous laughter and loud music greet us as we enter. The tavern floor is packed, brimming with patrons. The inside of the inn is dim and dingy, the air thick with the scent of stale ale and unwashed bodies. The floorboards creak under our feet as we make our way to the bar and ask for the barkeep.

A few of the patrons nearby cast suspicious glances our way but then quickly avert their gazes as Malak glares in their direction, his face half-obscured in shadow and his eyes blazing with anger.

The barkeep makes his way over, and a deep sense of

JESSICA GRAYSON & ARIA WINTER

unease settles in the pit of my stomach as he looks us over. "How can I help you?" he asks.

"We need a room," Malak says gruffly. He slaps five coins on the counter and the barkeeper's eyes light up with greed. "A discreet one," Mal says, and then gestures to me. "My mistress and I do not want to be disturbed, especially by my wife."

The innkeeper flashes a knowing wink at Mal. "Have no fear, good sir. If anyone shows up asking after you, I'll be sure to send them away."

Mal loops a possessive arm around my waist as he guides me through the rough-looking crowd and up the stairs to our room. The interior is just as dingy as the tavern below.

The walls are covered in two layers of chipped and different colored blue paint and the bed is missing one of its legs, with a stack of books holding it up. The hearth is nothing more than a few smoldering embers and the windows are so covered in grime, I can barely see anything outside. A tattered sofa sits before the hearth and Mal guides me to it.

He sits and then pulls me into his lap. "Rest, Luna, and I will keep watch. I'll wake you when it's time to leave."

"What about you?" I ask. "Are you not tired?"

He shakes his head. "I'll sleep when we reach the other side."

* * *

Mal's soft voice in my ear awakens me. "It's time, Luna," he whispers. "We must go."

Still groggy, I lift my head, rubbing my eyes. Mal kneels in front of me. He presses a tender kiss to my forehead. The fog of sleep lifts from my mind, and I'm instantly alert. Worry tightens my chest as I think of what we must do, but I push it back down.

Mal hands me a dagger. The blade is sharp, but the handle is worn as if from heavy use. "Where did you get this?" I ask, but his eyes give him away, so I amend my question. "When did you steal this?"

"An hour ago," he says. "I found it behind the bar."

"You're sure no one saw you?"

He dips his chin and then glances at the blade. "You know how to use this?"

I purse my lips. "Stab them with the pointy end?"

He chuckles and then pulls me into his arms.

"I have not forgotten the lesson you gave me when we were younger," I admonish. "Surely you remember how horrified my father was when I proudly displayed some of my defensive knife skills to him."

Mal laughs even harder. "I thought he would pass out from shock," he murmurs into my hair as he holds me close. "You are my heart, Luna. You are everything to me."

"I love you," I whisper.

He cups my face with both hands and stares deep into my eyes, his expression sobering. "Remember what I told you. If I tell you to run, you must run."

"I won't leave you," I state firmly. When he opens his mouth to argue, I force out the words. "Never again."

He swallows hard and takes both my hands in his. "I know you are still upset about what happened between us, but you must believe me, Luna. What I did, I did to protect you, and if I had to make the same choice again, I would."

Ice fills my veins. "Is that why you did not fully claim me in the cave?"

"What?"

"Because if you think it will protect me, you would leave me again."

"Luna, I—"

"Do not answer," I snap, pain and anger building deep within as the old wounds reopen that I thought had already healed. I turn my back to him, too angry to speak.

He slips his arms around my waist and pulls me back into his chest. My body instinctively melts into his solid warmth. "If we are separated, I will find you. I will not leave you again, Luna. The reason I did not claim you is because you are near the fertile peak of your cycle. I did not want to risk my seed taking root in your womb without discussing it with you first."

CHAPTER 21

MALAK

Inhaling sharply, she turns in my arms. "That's why you did not fully claim me?"

I nod.

Relief flashes behind her eyes. She stretches up on her toes and wraps her arms around my neck. "What if I want a child?"

"So soon?" I ask, searching her face.

She rests her forehead to mine. "We wasted three years apart, Mal. I want everything with you."

My inner wolf revels in her proclamation, and I lift her into my arms and press her back to the wall. "When we cross the bridge," I whisper between kisses. "I am taking you straight to the temple. We will marry according to the ways of your people, and I will claim you on the altar before the moon goddess."

The scent of her arousal fills the air, and I growl low in my throat. "I will take you many times, my beautiful mate."

"Is that a promise?" She grins.

I kiss her long and deep, sealing my vow.

When I pull back, I touch her face, staring deep into her eyes. "You will be a Princess of Winterhold and High Lady of the Vale. You will rule by my side as my mate and my equal. We will raise our family there, and we will have a beautiful life."

"What about your people?" she asks. "Are you sure they will accept me?"

"Ours is not the first Wolf-Shifter and human pairing since the end of the war. All wolves respect the mate bond. It is a sacred blessing from the moon goddess. And all pups created from such unions are born with the ability to shift; they are accepted into the packs without question. My people will accept you, and any pups we may have. I am certain of it."

She brushes her lips to mine, and whispers against them. "I cannot wait to start our life together, Mal."

"It is all I have dreamed of for so many years." Emotions lodge in my throat, but I manage to speak around them. "You are everything to me, my beautiful Luna. As soon as we cross the bridge into the Vale, I will do what I should have done three years ago. I will bind myself to you, and I will remain at your side until the day I draw my last breath."

She takes my hand, entwining our fingers. "Whatever happens, we will face the future together, Mal."

"Together," I reply solemnly.

* * *

WHEN WE REACH THE BRIDGE, I instruct Luna to climb onto my back.

"Won't we be spotted easier if—"

"We are going to climb underneath," I explain.

Her eyes widen as she gazes at the wide expanse between

the mountains and the long drop to the river below. She swallows hard. "Mal," she says, an edge of worry in her tone. "What if we fall?"

"We will not fall," I reassure her. "There are supports beneath that we can use."

She looks down at the gorge again. "You've... done this before?"

I shake my head.

"Then, how do you know it will work?"

"Because I've read reports of people crossing the bridge this way to get into the Vale undetected, to avoid the archers overhead."

"But if your warriors know of this, then will they not catch us?"

A grin tilts my lips. "When they discover us, we will have time to explain who we are."

Hesitantly, she climbs onto my back. Her worry pulses through the bond like an insistent drum as we approach the edge of the railing. The scent of her fear is thick in the air, but she does not complain. Instead, she holds tightly to me as I drop over the edge and onto a wooden support beam below.

CHAPTER 22

LUNA

The dull roar of the water far below us echoes loudly beneath the bridge. My pulse pounds in my ears as Mal carefully balances on one of the wooden support beams, with his arms outstretched on either side as I cling to him, remaining completely still.

I'm too afraid to do more than breathe shallowly, fearing I'll cause us to topple over the side and into the ravine.

A sharp whistling sound flies past us, and my heart stops when I realize it's an arrow. "Mal," I whisper urgently.

"I know," he grits through his teeth. "We are fine. Do not worry."

He quickens his pace, moving fast across the support beam until he reaches the safety of the first arch.

More arrows fly past us, many of them hitting the stone as we hide behind it. They're coming from the direction of Avalor. Voices shout overhead, echoing across the divide. A man's voice calls out, "If you surrender now, we will spare your life, Prince Malak! Prince Duren cares only for his betrothed! If you return her to him, he will be lenient with you!"

Mal and I both still a moment before he shouts back. "If you hit me with an arrow, Prince Duren's betrothed will fall with me!"

"Then, the prince will have no choice but to declare war against Winterhold and the Vale," he replies smoothly. "To avenge the capture and death of his beloved."

"I am not being held against my will," I call out. "I refuse to marry Prince Duren!"

"You are speaking under duress, child," the man shoots back. "Surrender now, and we might be inclined to spare your Wolf."

"They'll kill you, Mal," I whisper in his ear. "We cannot go back."

"You could die if we continue," he says.

"Then we will either live or die together," I state firmly. "I'm not leaving without you."

"You are my heart," he whispers.

"And you are mine," I reply softly. "Now, let's go."

"Hold tight to me," Malak says. Drawing in a deep breath, he breaks into a run, racing across the wooden supports so fast everything blurs around us. I close my eyes against a wave of nausea and dizziness, sending a prayer to the gods to grant us safe passage.

Arrows whistle past us, and my heart taps a frantic beat as I struggle to remain still and calm.

Mal jumps and my heart slams in my throat when I open my eyes as he catches the upper railing, and then hoists us up and over the side.

A contingent of soldiers carrying the banner of Winterhold march toward us, and I smile. "Winterhold is here, Mal. Ren sent the raven to your brother."

A unit of Vale warriors approaches from the side, halting

when they reach us.

I slide off Mal's back, and he takes my hand as a Winterhold soldier bows to us both.

"Your brother, King Fredrik, received word you needed aid," he says. "Vale is a territory of Winterhold and we are at your command, my Prince and High Lord." He bows low. "What would you have us do?"

"Defend the border," Mal says. "Allow no one to cross from Avalor until we have reached an accord with their king."

The guard dips his chin. "Of course, my Prince. Your brother asked me to inform you that he awaits you at the fortress."

Mal gives him a subtle nod and then turns to his Vale warriors. "Send someone ahead to retrieve my brother. Tell him to meet us at the temple."

The closest one bows and then leaves to do as commanded.

I squeeze Mal's hand, and he turns back to me. "You truly mean for us to get married right now?"

"Yes." He touches my face, studying me like I'm a rare and precious treasure. "I meant it when I said I do not want to wait any longer. You are my mate, and I want to seal you to me in the ways of your people and mine."

Happiness fills me. I want nothing more than to marry him, but not like this.

Reading my hesitation through the bond, he frowns. "What is wrong? Do you not want this?"

"I do," I reply quickly. "But"—I gaze down at my clothing—"I need a bath and a dress that is not in tatters."

He laughs softly and gathers me in his arms. He spins me around once before pressing a tender kiss to my lips as a handsome smile lights his face. "Then you shall have both, my beautiful mate."

CHAPTER 23

LUNA

al leads me to a smaller building beside the temple. It is made of the same smooth, white stone as the larger structure, but the outside is very plain in comparison. "What is this place?"

"This is where the priests and priestesses reside. There are quarters for visitors in here that we may use."

When we enter, a priest and a priestess each greet us with a subtle bow. Mal informs them of our request for a bath and fresh clothing before our ceremony, and they lead us to the guest rooms. The interior is stark but beautiful. The fireplace across the way has a roaring fire on the hearth and a sofa and two chairs before it. The walls are lined with shelves of ancient books and scrolls.

The floors are covered with thick, gray carpets and the windows have stained glass designs in the center while the rest of the pane is plain glass.

We walk down a narrow hallway, lined with windows

that look out onto an atrium, full of blooming vegetation. The priestess guides me to a room near the end and the priest guides Mal to the one beside it.

When I step inside, there is a small bed against one wall and a sofa in the center. Another door across the way opens into a cleansing room with a tub already filling with warm water.

The priestess studies me with piercing yellow eyes. "I am Felina. Forgive me, my Lady, but the only gowns we have are simple robes."

"That will be fine," I reply with a warm smile.

She bows and then leaves me to bathe.

When I am done, I change into a silver robe. For all that she insists it is simple, it is elegantly made. The material is soft as silk against my skin. Instead of buttons or fastenings, there is only a small sash that ties around my waist to secure the opening.

The priestess returns with a large bouquet of flowers, arranging them in a vase on a nearby table. "I thought you might wish to know that word is already spreading throughout the city that our High Lord has returned with his mate. The people of Bridgemore are leaving flowers outside the temple in honor of your ceremony."

I'm stunned by her words. "They do not care that I am human? From Avalor?"

Felina shakes her head. "You are the High Lords fated mate," she replies, as if that answers everything. "It is an honor to help prepare you for your ceremony, Lady Luna," she continues. "The High Lord is a brave and noble leader who saved us from the Troll invaders. It is no wonder that the people of the Vale would wish you both many blessings."

"Thank you," I reply, offering my best smile. It is good to know that Mal is so well-loved by his people, and to have the reassurance that that regard seems to extend to me as well.

While Felina helps me comb out my hair, I inquire about undergarments. She gives me a strange look. "I could… perhaps find something appropriate, but it will take time. Most do not wear anything beneath their robes."

"They don't?" I ask, confused. "Why not?"

"Most who come to the temple seek the blessing of the moon goddess upon their union," she says. "Hoping she will bless them with child when they worship at her altar."

My cheeks flare with heat when I realize what she means. It is the same reason Wolf-Shifters make love during the mating chase beneath the full moon. It is considered a form of worship, and they believe the goddess grants blessings when they do this.

Nervous excitement runs through me as I study myself in the mirror one last time. I have waited three years for this moment, and I do not want to wait any longer.

Felina guides me into the magnificent temple surrounded by towering walls of white stone. The ceiling above is lost in shadow, with shafts of soft light filtering in from the stained-glass windows, casting gorgeous patterns on the floor.

She leads me to an open garden in the heart of the massive structure. A beautiful oasis, surrounded by lush greenery and fragrant flowers. The air is filled with the soft rustling of leaves and the sweet scent of blooms. At the center is an altar, dedicated to the moon goddess.

It is crafted from gleaming white stone and adorned with intricate designs that shimmer in the soft glow of the moon-light. The altar is surrounded by candles, their flickering flames casting an ethereal light over the entire space.

As we approach the altar, a sense of awe and reverence pass over me.

Mal walks toward me, dressed in similar attire. His brother, Fredrik, comes up beside him, greeting me with a warm smile. "It has been too long since I've seen you, my friend," he says.

"You too," I reply softly.

He arches a brow. "I suppose I will have to address you as my sister now."

A beaming smile lights my face. "I would like that."

"I came as soon as I received Prince Renard's raven," he adds. "I am glad you are both well."

Mal smiles at me. "It seems you were right about the Fox Prince. He was true to his word."

Fredrik's gaze sweeps to mine. "I always felt that you would be part of our family someday, and I am glad that you found your way back to my brother."

Despite that he is king now, he was my friend first and foremost when we were younger. His acceptance of me now, even after our kingdoms went to war, touches me deeply. I step forward and give him a warm hug, pulling Mal into it as well.

"All is as it should be," Mal whispers.

"All is as it should be," Fredrik replies softly, and my heart aches for him. I only hope that he finds happiness, like ours, someday too.

* * *

THE PRIEST STANDING before us appears slightly disheveled. I suspect he was awakened much earlier than he is used to in order to perform this ceremony.

Mal slips his hands into mine, his palms callused but warm against my own. The top of my head barely reaches his chin. I gaze up at him, and his green eyes are fixed upon my own, love and happiness easily read behind them.

The priest instructs us to recite our human vows, and I'm

pleasantly surprised he is familiar with them. Mal's gaze holds my own as he vows to love, honor, and cherish me.

Anticipation thrums across our bond, and when the priest instructs Mal to kiss me, he captures my mouth in a claiming kiss.

When he pulls back, he looks to his brother and the priest. "Leave us," he says. "I wish to claim my mate in the old ways, in the presence of the goddess."

My cheeks flare with warmth at his words, even as heat pools low in my belly. As soon as everyone is gone, I turn to Mal. My heart hammers as his green eyes stare deep into mine. His face is so close, the warmth of his breath fans across my skin. His masculine scent surrounds me, and I lean in and gently brush my lips to his.

He opens his mouth, and his tongue finds mine. His kiss is soft, gentle and exploring at first before he cups the back of my head and takes control, tongue curling around my own as he kisses me like a man possessed.

A soft moan escapes me as he traces his hand down my body and cups my breast. I arch against him, and he rips his mouth from mine and trails a line of kisses across my jaw and down my neck.

He skims his nose along my sensitive flesh, inhaling deeply and then growling low. "Your scent calls to me," he murmurs against my skin. "If I take you now, there is a risk you will conceive. We can wait, and I can have one of the healers prepare the *arnai* tea to prevent—"

I press a finger to his lips. "No," I whisper. "I want you. I told you, Mal. I want everything with you."

Possessive fire burns in his eyes as I untie the sash of my robe. I slide it back from my shoulders and it falls to the grass, pooling at my feet.

His chest heaves as he draws in a shaking breath while his

heated gaze travels over my body. He removes his robe and I study his broad, muscular shoulders and the hard planes of muscle that line his abdomen and chest. His entire form is masculine perfection, like a statue carved in marble.

A low growl rumbles deep in his throat a moment before he loops his arm around my waist and pulls me to him. He dips his nose to the curve of my neck and shoulder, tracing his tongue over the mark on my neck.

"Mine," he growls and then moves his palm over my right breast. Gently, he squeezes the soft mound, and I arch against him with a low moan as he brushes his thumb over the sensitive peak.

"Mine to cherish," he whispers, trailing kisses down my neck. "Mine to touch." He grazes his fangs and traces his tongue lightly across my tender flesh as he moves down my body to my left breast. "Mine to love. Forever."

He closes his mouth over the soft globe, laving his tongue across the hardened tip.

A muffled groan escapes him as I thread my fingers through his hair and trace them over the pointed peaks of his ears.

He begins a gentle suction on my breast that makes me gasp, driving my desire even higher.

I've never wanted anything as much as I want him.

He turns his attention to the other breast then moves down my body. He lifts me onto the altar as if I weigh nothing, and then gently runs his hand up my inner thighs, parting me to his gaze.

He lifts a half-lidded gaze to me and his nostrils flare. "Your scent is intoxicating."

He guides my legs over his shoulders, and my heart pounds as he dips his head between my thighs and begins to feast. I moan as he drags his tongue through my already slick folds and reaches the small bundle of nerves at the apex.

"Mal," I breathe his name out like a prayer. "Feels so good."

He growls as I arch against him, concentrating his efforts on that small pearl of flesh, making me moan and writhe beneath him.

He bands an arm across my hips to hold me in place as he continues to lap at my folds, drawing out every bit of my pleasure as he teases his tongue over the area that makes my entire body light up with pleasure.

"Mal, please," I whimper, chasing my release.

I pull at his shoulders, trying to move him back up my body. I want this. I want him. And I don't want to wait any longer for him to fully claim me.

His eyes snap up to mine, full of heat. He presses a kiss to my inner thigh, and then moves up my body. I gasp as he slips one finger inside me, and arch into his hand as he inserts another. "I need you to come first, Luna, to help you take my knot, my beautiful mate."

He kisses me long and deep and then adds a third finger as his thumb traces over the sensitive bead of flesh between my thighs.

I wrap my legs around his waist and dig my nails into his back, holding on to him as pleasure coils tight in my core. "Mal," I whimper, and my entire body goes taut before I cry out his name as wave after wave of pleasure washes over and through me.

I'm still breathless and panting as he removes his fingers, and then notches the tip of his stav at my entrance. I look down my body. The shaft is long and thick. A milky bead of liquid gathers at the end.

His entire body is tense, muscles rippling like it's taking every bit of his control to remain still. "Are you certain?"

His gaze holds mine intensely. "Yes."

His eyes flash with hunger and a deep growl escapes him as he begins to push inside me.

The breath rushes from my lungs as he slowly enters me. Tight heat blooms deep in my core as my body stretches around his hardened length.

CHAPTER 24

MALAK

A low groan escapes me, and I fight against the temptation to spill inside her as I sink deep into her warm, wet heat. I want to give her pleasure first before I find my own release.

"So tight," I rasp, gritting my teeth as the base of my stav begins to heat with want to expand and knot deep within. But I must wait until I am fully sheathed.

A soft moan leaves her mouth as I advance. The tight clasp of her channel around my length is the most exquisite torture, and it takes every bit of control to keep from knotting immediately.

Luna tilts her hips, and I groan as I seat myself fully inside her. Primal instinct claws from deep within, my inner wolf demanding that I fill her with my essence. But I fight the urge to knot. I want to make her come first, softening her womb to accept my seed as I claim her.

Her entire form is soft and giving. She tightens her legs

around my waist, taking me deeper, and I begin to thrust inside her channel, losing myself in her body.

My name escapes her lips like a prayer as each stroke grows longer, deeper, and more forceful. I cannot get enough of my mate. My knot begins to expand, and she gasps. "What is—"

"My knot," I rasp.

CHAPTER 25

LUNA

H is knot expands deep inside me, almost to the point of pain, but not quite. I arch against his body, pleasure coiling low in my belly.

Locked together, I love the feel of his powerful body thrusting into mine. I trace my hands down the thick cords of muscle along his back, feeling them flex and bunch beneath my fingers as his hips move against my own. It's too much and not enough all at once. The delicious friction between us causing ripples of pleasure that expand deep in my core, building in intensity as I cling tightly to him.

The small muscles of my channel begin to flex and quiver around his length. I'm so close to the edge as each thrust becomes deeper and more forceful.

He growls and begins to move faster. My body tightens around his length as if trying to pull him even deeper.

With one arm banded around my waist, he grips my chin with the other, forcing my gaze to his. His eyes stare deep into mine, full of hunger, as he bares his fangs and growls. "You are mine, Luna."

My mouth falls open as a small pinch of pain is followed quickly by pleasure as his knot expands even more in my channel.

"Yes." I barely manage to breathe through my pleasure. "I'm yours."

He quickens his pace as he pumps into me. I've never felt so full. Everything around us falls away and it is only him and me. In this moment, we are one body, one mind, one heart, one soul.

He cups my breast and as his thumb brushes across the peak, it sends me spiraling over the edge into beautiful oblivion.

I cry out his name as I find my release and it triggers his own. His stav begins to pulse strongly in my channel and he releases a primal roar as intense heat erupts deep inside my core, filling me with the delicious warmth of his seed.

He leans in and the light sting of his fangs as he renews my mark is quickly replaced by pleasure as he fills me again. My channel clamps down hard around his length as another orgasm sweeps through me, this one stronger than the last, pulling his essence deep into my womb.

He wraps his arms around my body and pulls me from the altar, settling on his knees on the grass, holding me flush against his form before reaching up under my arms to grip my shoulders, pulling me to him as he continues to thrust up inside me.

Each movement of his body against mine only adding to the overwhelming sensations moving through me.

"Mine," he growls. Intense warmth blooms inside me, as he fills me again, sending me over the edge, waves of pleasure crashing through me.

It feels as though it goes on forever. His body is locked

with mine, and everything is so sensitive it's almost too much. Every nerve ending along my body where he touches and connects with me is ablaze with desire. I writhe in his grasp, as he erupts inside me again, holding me tightly to him.

"Malak," I barely manage. "It's so intense, I—"

My mouth falls open, and a moan parts my lips as my body tightens rhythmically around his length, drawing his seed deep into my womb.

I lose track of how many times we both come, each one more intense than the last. My heart is still pounding, and I'm panting heavily as he gently rolls us onto our sides, his length still knotted inside me.

He skims his nose along my neck, a low and possessive growl rumbling in his chest.

"That was... there are no words," I barely manage.

He seals his mouth over mine in a claiming kiss.

When his knot finally goes down, he carefully pulls away from my body. My inner thighs are slick with his release. I lie completely spent in his arms, the dull ache between my thighs reminding me that I've been thoroughly claimed. His stav is still hard against my abdomen.

He touches my cheek. "I must have you again, my Luna," he whispers softly.

My lips part on a breath, and I nod. He rolls me beneath him, settling between my thighs. His gaze holds mine, and the breath stutters from my lungs as he slowly pushes into me.

I wrap my legs tightly around him as he begins to stroke long and deep. Together, we fall over the edge several more times before I finally drift away to sleep in his arms.

CHAPTER 26

MALAK

Luna is still asleep when I wrap her up in her robe and carry her back to the temple guest rooms. We pass no one on the way there. Everyone is asleep and my guards are nearby, but far enough away to give us privacy.

Gently, I lay her down in the bed and then go out into the hallway. I call one of the guards over and instruct him to find my mate some clothing. A priestess appears a moment later with a parcel in hand.

She bows as she hands it to me. "I took the liberty of procuring a new dress and cloak, my Lord."

"Thank you," I reply, taking it from her.

As much as I want to let Luna sleep, it would be safer if we stay in the fortress just behind the temple. It's surrounded by an entire regiment of my warriors and those who have come with my brother from Winterhold.

No one should be able to cross the bridge without alerting my guards, but I'd be a fool to underestimate Prince

Duren's resolve. He believes Luna is key to his keeping the throne. He will not give up easily. He and his father need her to secure their power.

Gently, I take Luna's hand and press a tender kiss to her palm. Her eyelids flutter open and she gives me a sleepy smile. "You must dress," I whisper. "We need to go to the fortress."

Worry flits across her features and she sits up abruptly. "Why? What is wrong?"

"Nothing," I reassure her. "But the fortress is heavily guarded. We will be safer there until we can leave for the capital tomorrow."

I am anxious to get to the main castle, in the capital— Atheryn. It is less than a half day's journey from here.

When I first arrived in Vale, I had my Mage ward the entire palace and the surrounding grounds. Although my father distrusted most Mages, there were two he relied upon to protect Winterhold in the same manner.

It is the reason my family survived Avalor's assassination attempt. Without the wards to alert them of danger, I would have returned from Luna's country home to find my entire family slaughtered.

"All right," she replies, rising from the bed. "Let's go."

* * *

IT IS a short walk from the temple to the fortress, and I breathe a sigh of relief as we approach the entrance.

The fortress stands tall and proud at the edge of the city, the forest and the mountain spread out behind it. It guards the main road that winds through the woods to Atheryn.

It was built over a century ago by one of my ancestors to protect the capital and its people from invaders. Its gray stone walls stretch up toward the sky, offering a formidable barrier against those who would seek to breach its defenses.

Two guards open the large metal doors at the entrance, bowing low as we pass through. With Luna's arm looped through mine, we walk inside. Several of my warriors have gathered to show their respect, lining either side of the entryway. It is the first time I have visited as the new Lord of the Vale, and the first time they have seen their new Lady.

Captain Garen walks toward us. His sharp gray eyes study Luna at my side before he shifts his attention back to me. I fought with him in the war with Avalor, and I wonder how he will receive her. He had little love for her father, but he was always cordial to her when we were young.

To my pleasant surprise, he bows low and then straightens. "You honor us with your visit, my High Lord and my High Lady." He lifts his gaze to my mate. "It has been many years, Lady Luna. It is good to see you again."

She gives him a warm smile. "And you as well, Captain Garen."

He looks at me. "We have rooms prepared."

As he leads us through the wide hallways, he points out the various improvements that have been made to the fortress since he arrived a few months ago at his post. He points out the new storage for the growing armory and gestures out the window into the inner courtyard at the training grounds. Several warriors are out there, even now, sparring.

"The fortress is secure," Captain Garen says. "We will post two guards at your door at all times."

When we reach the guest rooms, I'm glad to note they are spacious and well-appointed, with plush bedding covered in white furs and stacked high with pillows, and a sofa with thick green cushions.

I'm about to close the door when Fredrik appears in the

doorway. I knew he was here, but I thought he would already be sleeping. "I hope I am not interrupting," he says.

"Not at all," Luna replies. "We just arrived."

He walks in and sighs heavily. "What is it?" I ask.

"Word has come from the bridge." He runs a hand roughly through his hair. "Prince Duren has convinced his father that Luna is being held against her will. The king is demanding her return, and Avalor is threatening war if you do not comply. Duren's army is camped on the Avalor side of Bridgemore."

CHAPTER 27

LUNA

"**D**oes he truly believe he will win?" Mal asks incredulously. "It has not been very long since we won the war and killed the former king and his son." He loops his arm around my waist and tugs me into his side. "Luna is my mate. If Duren dares think he will take her from me, I will end him."

"Duren knows I am not held against my will," I add. "He saw me leave with Mal. The war drained the royal treasury's reserves and there are many who question the new king's claim to the crown. That is why Duren and his father need my surname and my dowry to both legitimize and hold their positions on the throne."

Fredrik narrows his eyes. "If they want war, they will be facing both the armies of Winterhold and the Vale."

"There may be another way." Mal turns to him. "I will meet Duren on the bridge tomorrow. I will challenge him to fight me, sparing our armies. Surely his honor will not let him refuse this."

"If you kill him, his father may declare war anyway," I tell him.

"It is a risk we must take," Mal replies. He turns to me. "Wait here, where it is safe. I must go speak with our warriors."

"I'll come with you," I tell him.

"No," he says. "You are the one Duren wants. It is safer for you to remain here, under guard."

I open my mouth to argue, but he takes my hands and gives me a pleading look. "Please, Luna. I need to know you are safe and protected."

"That may be so, but I am your mate, and the High Lady of the Vale now. What kind of leader would I be if I did not go with you to face down my own people?" Resignation flashes in his eyes. "You know I'm right, Mal."

I give Fredrik a pointed look, and he claps a hand on Mal's shoulder. "She has a point."

Mal growls. "If she were your mate, would you knowingly place her in danger?"

Fredrik recoils as if struck. It is easy to see he still carries the pain of the deception of the blood witch that ensorcelled him. "Forgive me," Mal says quickly. "I did not mean to bring up—"

"You are right," Fredrik says a bit hesitantly. "I would not." He turns his gaze to me. "But that does not make Luna wrong either. The Avalor warriors are her people. They are here under their king's banner because they believe she has been taken against her will. If she is not there to refute this, they have only your word. The word of a Wolf that was once their enemy in battle. The same Wolf who helped to defeat their kingdom in war."

Mal cups my cheek and stares deep into my eyes. "You are everything to me. I only want to protect you."

I place my hand over his and lean into his touch. "I know.

But these are my people. Fredrik is right. They will not believe you. If I do not address them, they will believe the lies Duren has spread, and they will fight, and people will die. Perhaps even you." I press a tender kiss to his palm. "You have protected me. Now, it is time for you to let me protect you."

He pulls me into an embrace. "All right. But if things go badly, I want you to retreat to the fortress. Do you understand?"

I give him the answer he wants and nod softly. In truth, I would never leave his side. No matter what. We live together, or we die together. I'll not be separated from him again.

* * *

My nerves are a tangle of worry as we walk toward the bridge. The Vale warriors march on either side of us and those from Winterhold walk behind them, in a show of respect for the Vale's sovereignty but also a display of solidarity among the two territories.

Several of the businesses and homes we pass are closed and their windows boarded up in case of war. During the conflict between Avalor and Winterhold, the people of the Vale suffered twice over. During that time, their enemies lay just across the shared bridge and from the North the Trolls invaded, taking advantage of Winterhold's distraction to take over this smaller territory.

I only pray that war is not the outcome today. Not just for the Vale, but for my people as well. So many suffered and lived under fear for so long, I would not see those days returned.

When we approach the bridge, Avalor's banners wave in the distance. A golden sun against a white background.

The Vale's are almost a mirror of Winterhold's, with a

white wolf against a black banner, while Winterhold's has a dark wolf against royal blue.

Prince Duren sits upon his horse, dressed in finely polished armor that appears to have seen little use in battle.

Straightening my shoulders, I tip my chin high as I stand beside my mate, staring across at the warriors who have come believing they are here to free me from my captors.

"Why are you here, Duren?" Malak calls out. "And why have you brought an army to my borders?"

Duren urges his horse forward and gives him an imperious look. "I demand the return of my betrothed, Lady Luna of Avalor. Release her to me, or there will be war."

"There is no need for war, Prince Duren." I step forward, my voice ringing loud and clear across the divide. "I am here of my own volition, as you well know. And I would not see these brave warriors of Avalor—my own countrymen—give their lives for a cause you know to be false."

Although he is across the bridge, it is easy to read the anger that flashes across Duren's face. He turns his horse to his men, pronouncing loudly. "The Lady says these things for fear of her life, I am sure."

"No, I do not," I state firmly. "Prince Malak of Winterhold, Lord of the Vale, is my mate and my husband. I have chosen him and rejected you. Now, go home, Prince Duren, and do not allow your wounded pride to be the cause of these good men's deaths."

Duren's chest heaves as he levels a dark glare at me. Not to be deterred, he calls out to his men. "The Lady has been bewitched. She knows not what she says."

Malak bristles beside me, and a low growl rises from Fredrik's throat behind us.

"If you are so eager to fight, Prince Duren, I suggest we settle this in the old way." Mal steps forward. "I challenge you to combat by champion."

I inhale sharply, but remain still, not wanting to betray my worry. I know Mal is the better fighter, but I've seen highly trained fighters felled by a lesser opponent before.

After a moment's consideration, Duren turns to his men. "Which of you will fight for your kingdom to save—"

"I *said*," Malak growls, cutting him off. "*I* challenge *you*." Duren's head snaps back and Mal pins him with an angry glare. "Unless you are too cowardly to fight me."

Panic flits briefly across his features before they settle into a scowl. "I am the prince of Avalor, and I am no coward, Wolf," he sneers, dismounting his horse. "I accept upon one condition."

"What is it?" Mal asks.

"You fight me in your two-legged form at all times."

"Done."

CHAPTER 28

MALAK

L una's fear is palpable between the bond, but she hides it behind a stoic mask. Tears brighten her eyes, but she does not allow them to fall as she cups my cheek and stares deep into my eyes.

I open my mouth to reassure her of my victory, but she cuts me off. "I have no doubt you will win, Mal." She stretches up on her toes, presses her lips to mine, and then whispers against them. "Now, hurry and come back to me."

"Always," I reply softly.

I turn from her, and Fredrik hands me a sword. His gaze holds mine intently as he dips his chin, and I head for the bridge.

A bitter wind sweeps up from the canyon below, whipping at my form as I head for the center of the bridge.

Prince Duren approaches from the opposite end, anger etched in his features. It seems the prince of Avalor is upset that I challenged him in front of his men, and now he thinks he will make me pay for it.

Tension crackles like a thunderstorm between us as we face off. The sound of metal rings through the canyon as we draw our swords, and then begin circling, sizing each other up.

My heart pounds in my chest, anticipation pumping through my veins. He dared threaten to take Luna from me, and I will show him how a Wolf defends his mate.

I grip my sword tighter, focusing all my attention and rage upon this pompous prince, snarling as his eyes meet mine.

He lunges forward, blade flashing through the air. Our swords meet with a thunderous clash, echoing through the canyon as we begin.

To my great surprise, his skill and strength are nearly even with mine, but I know I must be the one to win this day. Determination drives me forward, striking with all my might, determined to defeat my opponent and claim victory.

Duren strikes low in an attempt to catch me off guard, but I easily dodge to the side, avoiding the attack. I counter with a swift strike, but Duren blocks it with his sword.

The clang of metal against metal fills the air as we engage in a heated exchange of blows. Duren is good, but I am the better warrior, moving as one with my sword until it becomes an extension of my own body.

Duren's eyes widen as this realization sinks in. The stench of his fear touches my nostrils and I know victory is nearly mine for he is already losing the battle in his mind.

Desperate to gain the upper hand, he jabs at my eyes, but I twist away at the last moment. The sun breaks through the clouds, reflecting off his polished armor with blinding intensity. Sensing an opportunity, he rips off his chest plate, aiming the light directly at my eyes. I blink, trying to focus, and he takes advantage of my temporary distraction and swings his sword, slicing across my arm.

Sharp pain rips through my shoulder and I stumble back, barely managing to catch myself before I fall. I recover quickly as rage sharpens my focus. Snarling, my wolf instincts take over, anger fueling my movements as I renew my attack.

Duren's eyes are full of panic as I relentlessly push forward until he stumbles back against the railing. Gritting my teeth, I place my blade at his throat, ready to end him if he so much as breathes wrong.

He stares up at me, anger easily read in his features.

"Do you surrender?" I growl.

He hesitates a moment before finally dipping his chin in a quick nod.

I turn away from him, and Luna rushes toward me. She leaps into my arms, and I catch her, spinning her around once before capturing her mouth in a claiming kiss. "I knew you would win." She smiles against my lips. "I had no doubt that you could beat—"

"Look out!" Fredrik's voice cuts through the air.

Sharp pain arcs across my back, and I spin to find Duren standing before me, his chest heaving with unbridled rage and a bloodied knife in his hand.

Warmth spreads across my right shoulder and down my spine. A deep growl rumbles in my chest, and my claws lengthen. If he thinks he can end me so easily, he is sorely mistaken.

I step toward him, but Luna is faster. She lunges for the knife, gripping his wrist. He's so shocked, it takes him a moment to realize what is happening, and before he can react, she twists, using the weight of her body to knock him off balance, plunging the knife deep into his chest.

His mouth falls open in shock as a crimson stain blooms across his chest before dripping down his body to pool on the ground at his feet. He drops to his knees and blood gurgles from his mouth as he tries to speak before he falls forward, face down.

Everyone stares in shock as Luna stands over him. Her hands are shaking, and she releases the blade. It falls to the stone with a sharp clang that rings across the canyon. I gather her up in my arms and turn her to face me. "Are you all right?"

She blinks several times as if coming back to herself. "What about you?" she asks in concern. "You're bleeding, Mal."

I shrug. "It's a flesh wound. It will heal."

Still in shock, she huffs out a puff of air in a small laugh and shakes her head. She wraps her arms around me and hugs me close. "You are truly well?" she whispers in my ear, her voice shaking. "Tell me the truth."

"I promise. I am not going to die."

"You'd better not," she says, peppering my face with kisses. "If you die, I'll never forgive you."

"Then I suppose I'll have to live forever." I huff out a laugh.

My mate is brave, strong, and selfless. The warriors of Vale and Winterhold will remember this day. I tighten my arms around her and gently nuzzle her hair. She will be a fierce and excellent mother to our pups.

Fredrik claps a hand on my shoulder, and I hiss at the contact. I may not be dying, but my wound does ache something fierce.

I growl low, and he grins. "Oh, stop. You are fine."

I narrow my eyes. Despite my attempt to hide it, a slight grin tilts my lips.

Gently, I set Luna on her feet and turn to face the soldiers of Avalor. "You witnessed my victory in trial by combat as well as your leader's attempt to kill me once it was done." I allow my gaze to sweep over them. "Go home, and let there be no more blood spilled between us this day or any other. As you can see, my mate, Princess Luna of Winterhold, and Lady of the Vale, is not here against her will. Your intentions, although misguided by your own prince, were honorable, and I'll not hold it against you for coming to the defense of Lady Luna when you thought she was held against her will."

The men stare at me, and I brace myself, wondering if they will accept my words or if war between us is inevitable.

Luna takes my hand as she addresses them. "Warriors of Avalor, your prince brought you here under false pretenses." She raises our joined hands. "I chose Prince Malak as my husband and my mate. There is no need for any more blood to spill needlessly. You are honorable men, who deserve a life of peace. Go home to your families."

One of Duren's men steps forward. Judging by the insignia on his armor, he is a general. He removes his helmet, revealing dark hair streaked through with white. His piercing brown eyes meet mine briefly before he bows low to Luna. "We accept the outcome of the challenge by combat. The victory goes to the Vale, and we will return home and report to our King that you are well, Lady Luna."

She dips her chin. "Go with my blessing. Return to your king and tell him that if he doubts anything of my claim, he may come see me himself, and I will reassure him that I am well."

CHAPTER 29

LUNA

Fredrik sits beside me as we observe the healer tending to Malak's wound. There's so much blood, I have a hard time believing it is not a serious injury.

"Our kind heal quickly, Luna," Fredrik reassures me. "He will be fine. Trust me."

The healer continues to run her hands over his wound, and I watch in awe as the torn tissue begins to reknit before my very eyes.

"I must draft a message to Avalor—to King Branac," Fredrik says, drawing my attention back to him. "I would appreciate your help with the wording of it. I would prefer to avoid another war if we can."

"Fortunately, there were many witnesses," I tell him. "Duren's men saw his dishonorable actions near the end. There is no defense for what he did. And it was not Malak that killed him." I swallow thickly as worry creeps down my spine. "If anything, the king will direct his hatred at me."

Fredrik turns to me. "You are family, Luna. As much my

sister as Malak is my brother. All is as it should be. As it should have been three years ago," he adds before his expression hardens. "But if King Branac thinks to find justice by threatening you in any way, he will have the armies of Winterhold and the Vale at his doorstep."

I swallow around the knot of emotion in my throat as I meet his gaze. "Thank you."

"You do not need to thank me. You are family. I am glad that you and Malak found your way back to each other." He smiles, but it is easy to read the sadness behind his eyes. "Truly."

Although I know I probably should not bring it up, I cannot help it. "Mal told me what happened to you, with the Blood Witch."

"I was a fool." He stares down at his hands. "I did things that I am not proud of."

"You were under a dark spell," I remind him. "You must forgive yourself."

"I tell myself that I should have known. But when I met her, she seemed... perfect." He sighs heavily. "I was always jealous of you and Malak. Not because I desired you as mine," he quickly adds, "but because I knew even back then what you were to each other, and I wanted something like that. The bond you two shared, while we were growing up, was plain for all to see."

"Perhaps you will find what you are looking for, Fredrik," I offer.

"I gave the Blood Witch my bond," he says sadly. "And even though the healers claim that it was never truly formed... it felt real to me at the time. I do not know that I could ever give of myself in that way to another."

I hate seeing Fredrik hurt. He is a good man. He doesn't deserve what happened to him. So, I offer the only comfort I can. "The heart is stronger than many believe," I speak softly.

"It can be easily broken, but it can also heal. And when it does, it becomes even stronger than it was before." I pause. "The hardest part is entrusting it into someone's care again." I allow my gaze to drift to Mal. "But it is worth the risk."

"And what if it all goes badly again?" Fredrik asks, his expression more vulnerable than I have ever seen him before. "What then?"

"It is a risk, and only you can decide if you wish to try. The alternative is to be alone," I explain. "And while that may be preferable to some, I knew it was not so for me."

"Malak never stopped loving you, Luna. I was there. I know it to be truth. You must never doubt it."

"I know that now."

A pair of strong hands come to rest on my shoulders, and I lift my gaze to find Malak smiling down at me.

"I am completely healed now, my mate," he says, turning his back just enough that I can see the thin line of his scar where he was injured. "See?"

He pulls me to my feet and loops his arms around my waist, surrounding me with his tall, muscular form. I wrap my arms around his waist, snuggling into his solid warmth.

"I have a request," Fredrik says, calling our attention back to him.

"What is it?" I ask.

"If your firstborn pup is male, perhaps you might consider naming him Fredrik." He grins teasingly. "After all, I will be his favorite uncle, will I not?"

Mal growls low, and I laugh as I reply. "We'll have to think about it and get back to you."

"Good," he says, flashing his fangs in a wide smile. "I would like to bring Mother to visit you both at winter solstice," he adds, his expression falling a bit. "If it is all right with you, Luna."

I look up at Mal. "Mother helped me persuade father to

stop looking for your family. She knew what you were to me, and she did not wish to see you hurt. She merely worried that because you were human, our bonding would not be as strong as it would have been if you were a Wolf-Shifter." He cups my chin, brushing his thumb across my lower lip. "She was wrong."

I turn back to Fredrik. "We would be glad to have you both. Will you be accompanying us to the capital tomorrow?"

He shakes his head. "I must return to Winterhold, but I will visit as soon as I am able."

Part of me is nervous, but also excited to travel to the capital. I've never been to Atheryn, but I have heard tales of its beauty. And I can hardly wait to see my new home, and begin my new life with my mate.

CHAPTER 30

LUNA

We have been traveling for nearly half a day. Mal and I were sad to say goodbye to Fredrik this morning, but he has promised to visit us during winter solstice. The sun hangs low in the sky by the time we draw near to the capital. Mal's voice whispers in my head as we approach a bend in the road. *"On the other side of this, you will be able to see Atheryn, and the castle."*

I lean forward, resting my face against the thick fur of his neck and shoulder to hug him. "I can hardly wait."

A rumbling growl of approval vibrates in his chest, and he turns his head back to me, nudging me lightly with his snout. *"We will arrive in time for the harvest festival, and the mating chase."*

Heat pools low in my belly as he continues. *"I will claim you in the ways of my people, so that none doubt that you are mine."*

A smile crests my lips. "I do not believe anyone doubts that, my love."

He glances back at the long line of warriors following us in their shifted forms as well. *"There are too many unmated males among my guards. My inner wolf will not be settled until I have claimed you in the chase."*

Softly, I bite my lower lip and speak to his mind. "I cannot wait."

We round the bend, and my first glimpse of Atheryn takes my breath away. The towering castle is built into the side of a mountain, with the city spread out in the valley before it. Its walls are made of gray stone, awash in beautiful colors of oranges, pinks, and purples as the sun sets behind the mountain. It stands tall and proud, adorned with towers and battlements. The banners of Vale—the white wolf against a black background—wave back and forth in the wind.

A waterfall cascades down the mountain and along the side of the castle before flowing into a river that winds through the center of the city.

The buildings are made of gray and white stone. Smoke rises from the chimneys along the peaked, dark rooftops. Golden light spills out of the windows onto the streets from the shops and houses. The air filled with the sounds of laughter and chatter as people gather together to celebrate the harvest festival.

As we make our way through the city, the people cheer the return of their Lord and their warriors, lining up to observe as we pass. When we reach the city center, Malak halts and then lowers himself so that I may slide off his back.

He shifts instantly into his two-legged form, and so do the rest of the warriors. He takes my hand and then turns to address the growing crowd. "People of Vale, I present to you my mate—my fated one," he says pointedly. "Princess Luna of Winterhold and High Lady of the Vale."

The crowd erupts in more cheers of jubilation. I worried

that I would be met with suspicion because I am human, but I am glad to know that I was wrong.

When we reach the castle, I am awestruck by the grandeur and beauty of this place. The walls are adorned with tapestries and paintings depicting nature scenes with wolves. The floors are made of polished stone, their surfaces reflecting the light from the high windows.

The servants greet us, their eyes alight with something akin to intense fascination when Mal introduces me as his fated one. He told me before that this was sacred among Wolf-Shifters and it is easily read in their features as they observe in awed silence as we pass.

Our footsteps echo as Mal leads me up a grand staircase. He guides me down a hallway to a set of large double doors. "These are our rooms," he says, pushing them open.

The bedroom is spacious and elegant, with a high, canopied bed swathed in silken white sheets with a black comforter. The sigil of the wolf threaded through the fabric in silver. The walls are adorned with more tapestries, depicting wolves and hunting scenes. The windows are tall and arched, letting in the last of the light, as day turns to night. The full moon is visible, rising in the distance.

The cleansing room is equally impressive, with a large pool carved into the floor. The soft scent of lavender and roses fills the air, and as I gaze at the pool of crystal clear water, I notice steam rising from the surface. "It is fed by a warm spring beneath the castle," Mal says, answering my unspoken question. "It is continually refreshed."

The walls are tiled in gleaming stone, and there is a sink and mirror for grooming and a lavatory behind another door.

"Does it please you?" Mal asks softly behind me.

I turn and wrap my arms around his neck, smiling up at him. "It's beautiful."

A devastatingly handsome smile curves his mouth. "I have one more surprise."

I arch a brow. "What is it?"

"Rest first, while I take care of a few things, and I will return as soon as I can."

Although I want to argue that I'm not tired, I would love a bath. Especially after traveling most of the day. So, I nod.

* * *

WHEN I'M FINISHED BATHING, I change into a sleep gown left for me on the bed by one of the servants. I step back out into the bedroom and find a woman waiting.

She is dressed in a simple, gray tunic dress and pants. Her hair is brown and threaded through with white. Her golden-brown eyes study me before she bows low. She gestures to the table beside her and the tray for tea. "I am Kalina. It is lovely to finally meet you, my High Lady. I have heard much about you."

"You have?"

"One of your scouts returned early to the capital," she explains. "The entire city is already abuzz with the story of how you saved the High Lord's life from the dishonorable Prince Duren." A smile curves her mouth. "Word has spread that you are as fierce and brave as our High Lord."

I'm pleased, but a bit stunned by the knowledge that the people already hold me in such high regard. Before I can respond, she adds, "It is an honor to serve one as brave as you," she says. "Is there anything I can get you, my High Lady?"

We stopped to eat on the way here, so I am neither hungry nor thirsty. I am simply eager to see my mate again. "Do you know if the High Lord will return soon?" I ask.

"He should be here momentarily," she replies. "It is my

understanding he is simply ensuring that the palace and the grounds are well-protected."

Worry ripples down my spine. "Has he received word of some sort of danger?"

"No. But you are a newly mated pair. It is his instinct to want to ensure you are safe and secure." A wistful smile crests her lips. "I remember what it was like when my mate and I were newly bonded. And when I was carrying our pups, he was so overprotective he nearly drove me mad."

She bows again. "I am honored to meet you, my High Lady, and honored to serve in your household. If you need anything, please do not hesitate to let me know."

"Thank you, Kalina."

When she leaves, I feel lighter after having talked with her. My worries about being a human among Wolf-Shifters have been completely put to rest. I'm sure there will still be some who will not like having a human High Lady, but Mal's warriors and most of the house staff have been nothing but courteous to me.

I wrap a fur-lined robe around my shoulders and step out onto the balcony. The air is cool, but not uncomfortably so. I suspect it will be much colder up here when winter arrives, however.

I'm pleased to note the balcony overlooks a beautiful garden, full of lush greenery, vibrant flowers and trees that stretch tall and proud toward the night sky.

Strong arms encircle my waist, pulling me back against the solid warmth of Mal's chest. He leans in and nuzzles my neck, scenting me as a low growl leaves his throat. "You smell delicious," he rumbles.

I turn in his arms to face him. "I'm ready for my surprise."

He laughs and tugs me to his chest. He hoists me into his arms. "Hold tightly to me."

I only have a moment to loop my arms around his neck before he jumps from the balcony to the gardens below.

"Close your eyes," he whispers, and I do as he instructs.

He walks for a bit, and when he finally halts, he whispers again. "Now, open them."

I do as he commands and smile at the entrance to the hedge maze before us. "We have our own hedge maze?" I ask in wonder.

He nods. "Long ago, the Vale used to be a summer retreat for the royal family of Winterhold," he explains. "This garden and the maze were a gift from my great-grandfather to my great-grandmother."

Carefully, he lowers me to my feet. The full moon overhead provides just enough illumination that I can see clearly. Memories flood my mind and happiness blooms in my chest

as I smile over my shoulder. "Catch me if you can," I yell as I take off, sprinting down the path and around a sharp corner.

A thrill of excitement hums in my veins as Mal releases a low howl and then I hear his footsteps crunching along the path as he chases after me.

CHAPTER 31

MALAK

I race through the hedge maze, my heart pounding with excitement as I chase after my beautiful Luna. Her lovely red hair is flying behind her as she dashes down one path and then another.

My inner wolf claws and howls beneath the surface, thrilled by the hunt as my every sense sharpens, attuned to my mate, as I allow my primal instincts to overtake me.

Up ahead, Luna stumbles, and I pounce, scooping her up in my arms and twirling her around. She laughs, her eyes shining with delight, and I can't help but lean in to capture her lips in a kiss.

As our lips meet, the world around us fades away, and I am lost in the warmth of her embrace. Her soft curves press against me, her arms wrapped around my neck, and I am filled with a surge of love and desire, completely in her thrall.

She pushes away, laughing as she scrambles to race farther into the maze. Her escape calls forth something dark and primal deep within me as I race after her, holding back long enough to allow her to reach the altar to the moon goddess in the center of the maze.

I quicken my pace and wrap my arm around her waist, pulling her to my chest. With her back pressed to my front, I lean in and inhale deeply of her delicious scent of apples and cinnamon.

She moans as I kiss a line from her jaw down to her neck, leaning her head against my shoulder and pushing back against me.

Unable to hold back any longer, I spin her around and lift her into my arms. I walk her back to the altar and set her down on the edge. Without hesitation, I slice a line down the front of her gown, baring her to my gaze. I drop to my knees and then grip her thighs, opening her to me.

"Mal, I—"

The words die in her throat as I dip my head between her thighs and drag my tongue through her already slick folds. A rumbling growl escapes me as I taste of her essence. "Mine," I snarl and then begin to feast upon my mate.

She digs her heels into my shoulders, moaning my name as I tease my tongue through her sensitive flesh. Her entire body goes taut and then she cries out as she reaches her climax, flooding my tongue with her sweet nectar.

Her taste stokes the fires of my need, and I bear her to the ground and flip her onto her hands and knees. Using my claws, I slice away the last of her clothing, leaving her completely bare. I push her knees apart and then settle between them.

I notch myself at her entrance, and a low groan escapes me as I sink deep into her warm, wet heat. "So tight," I rasp as I lean forward. Covering her with my body, I rest my hands over hers, threading our fingers as I roll my hips.

She moans, and I clamp my teeth over the mark on her neck, not enough to break the skin but enough to hold her in place as I thrust into her. "More," she breathes, and I quicken my pace.

Pleasure ripples down my spine as my knot expands deep within, locking us together. The small muscles of her channel tighten around me, as if trying to draw me even deeper.

"You are mine," I growl. "Mine to cherish, mine to touch, mine to love forever."

"Yours," she agrees. "And you are mine."

Wrapping my arms around her waist, I pull her back, settling on my heels, and holding her flush against my body. With one arm around her chest, I palm the soft globe of her breast, massaging the sensitive peak as she leans back against me.

It is the fertile peak of her cycle. Her tantalizing scent calls to my inner wolf; he growls and thrashes beneath the surface, the instinct to breed her a primal need I cannot ignore.

I band my other arm around her hips, cupping her mons possessively and tracing my finger across the sensitive pearl of flesh between her folds as I thrust up into her body.

Her body tightens around mine and then clamps down on my stav as she reaches her climax.

"Mine," I roar as my stav erupts deep in her core, filling her with my seed.

* * *

As WE LIE in the grass, my knot is still buried inside her channel. I pull Luna against me, listening to the soft sounds of her breathing as she lies in my arms, fully sated and drifting in that space between sleep and wakefulness.

I rest my hand on her lower abdomen, and she places hers atop mine. "Do you think we—"

Her words cut off on a gasp as my stav erupts inside her again, and she moans my name as she finds her release.

I nuzzle her neck, grazing my fangs along her claiming mark. I have no doubt she will be carrying our pup before the next full moon. Especially after I take her again during the mating chase tomorrow night.

EPILOGUE

MALAK

I stand proudly beside my beautiful mate as the priestess settles a golden circlet crown atop her head. It is similar to mine, with a wolf sigil and moonstone in the center, matching the design of the wolf on the ring I gave her so very long ago.

Luna's grandmother observes her crowning with tears of happiness in her eyes. She has recently moved into the castle. I am glad that she agreed to live here with us as it pleases my mate immensely.

Luna smiles, and I pull her into my arms, pressing a tender kiss to her lips. My nostrils flare as her delicious scent blooms in the air around us. I lean in and skim the tip of my nose along her neck and then still. Happiness tightens my chest, and my inner wolf growls low as fierce protectiveness floods my veins.

The urge to snarl and snap at every person in the room is nearly overwhelming, and although I know it is only instinct to protect one's mate when they are with pup, I am having trouble forcing my inner wolf to settle.

A hand claps my shoulder, and I bite back a low growl as I turn to find my dear friend, King Henrick, behind me. He runs a hand through his short, pale blond hair as glowing blue eyes search mine. After a moment, he arches a brow. "I know that look," he says in a voice so low I'm sure no one else heard it. "Your mate is with child, is she not?"

Of course the Bear Shifter King would recognize this. I glance at his human mate, Queen Anna, beside him, her hand resting on her lower abdomen, carrying their cub.

"It is difficult," he murmurs. "The instinct to protect my mate and unborn cub is so great, if I could, I would keep Anna locked away in our rooms."

"Luna does not know yet," I whisper. "I only just realized this moment."

A faint smile curves his mouth. "Then, I will wait to congratulate you formally."

I turn back to Luna and I lean in to whisper that I wish to go somewhere private to talk, but Henrick's mate, Anna, walks over to her, her hazel eyes regarding my mate warmly. "It is lovely to meet you, Luna. I am glad you and Malak found your way back to each other."

She gestures to the table before us and a large, wrapped package on top. "We brought you a gift."

Luna carefully unwraps the paper and then gasps as it falls away. It is a perfect marble replica of the ice statue in Henrick's palace that I had made of Luna. I remember how sad I was when I carved it when I went to visit Henrick. It was the only place I could keep something to remember her without my father knowing that I still loved her.

Luna frowns. "How did you make this?"

"We had an artist copy the one Malak carved from ice that sits in the palace gardens." Anna smiles. "I have prayed to the goddess every day since I learned of your story that she would bring you back to each other."

Luna turns to me, tears in her eyes. "You made a statue of me?"

Emotions lodge in my throat, but I somehow manage to speak around them. "I missed you."

She hugs me close and whispers in my ear. "I missed you too." She turns to Anna and takes both her hands. "It is a lovely gift. Thank you so much."

Anna smiles. "Of course."

As the night wears on, I find it difficult to pull Luna away from Anna. It seems they are on the path to becoming good friends, and I am glad.

When I ask Luna to dance, she stands from her chair and then starts to fall back. I catch her before she falls, steadying her with my hand beneath her elbow. Her cheeks are slightly pale as she raises a shaking hand to her forehead. "I—I don't know what came over me. I—"

"Are you with child?" Anna asks, and Henrick and I go still.

Luna's gaze sweeps to me, and I give her a wolfish grin.

Her mouth drifts open as she stares up at me. "Are you sure?"

"Your scent has changed." I tap the side of my nose. "I am certain."

A beaming smile lights her face, and she throws her arms around my neck. I catch her around the waist and spin her around once before setting her back down. I drop my forehead gently to hers.

A tear slips down her cheek, and I brush it away with my thumb. "What is wrong?"

Her lovely eyes search mine. "Tell me this is real. That I have not dreamed all of this and I'll wake up and you'll be gone."

"This is real," I speak softly. "I am here, and I will never be parted from you again." I rest my palm on her lower abdomen, marveling at the knowledge that she is carrying our pup. She places her hand over mine and I brush my lips to hers. "You are mine, Luna. Always."

ALSO BY JESSICA GRAYSON

Next book in series : Charmed by the Fox Prince: A Rapunzel Retelling

If you enjoyed this book please leave a review on Amazon and/or Goodreads.

-Jessica Grayson

Of Fate and Kings Series

Bound to the Dark Elf King

Claimed by the Dragon King

Taken by the Fae King

Stolen by the Wolf King

Captured by the Orc King

Check out some of my other books while you're here.

Do you like Fairy Tale Retellings?

Fairy Tale Retellings (Once Upon a Fairy Tale Romance Series)

Taken by the Dragon: A Beauty and the Beast Retelling

Captivated by the Fae: A Cinderella Retelling

Rescued By The Merman: A Little Mermaid Retelling

Bound To The Elf Prince: A Snow White Retelling

Claimed By The Bear King: A Snow Queen Retelling

Protected By The Wolf Prince: A Red Riding Hood Retelling

Charmed by the Fox Prince: A Rapunzel Retelling

Of Gods and Fate (Greek God Romance Series)

Rescued: Fae Alien Romance

Stolen: Werewolf Romance

Taken: Vampire Alien Romance

Fated: Dragon Shifter Romance

Protected: Dragon Shifter Romance

Want Dragon Shifters? You can dive into their world with this completed Duology.

Mosauran Series (Dragon Shifter Alien Romance)

The Edge of it All

Shape of the Wind

V'loryn Series (Vampire Alien Romance)

Lost in the Deep End

Beneath a Different Sky

Under a Silver Moon

V'loryn Holiday Series (A Marek and Elizabeth Holiday novella takes place prior to their bonding)

The Thing We Choose

V'loryn Fated Ones (Vampire Alien Romance)

Where the Light Begins (Vanek's Story)

For information about upcoming releases Like me on

Facebook at Jessica Grayson

http://facebook.com/JessicaGraysonBooks.

OR

sign up for upcoming release alerts at my website:

Jessicagraysonauthor.com